TORN FROM TROY

Torn from Troy

ODYSSEY OF A SLAVE

Patrick Bowman

RONSDALE PRESS

TORN FROM TROY
Copyright © 2011 Patrick Bowman

RONSDALE PRESS
3350 West 21st Avenue, Vancouver, B.C., Canada V6S 1G7
www.ronsdalepress.com

Typesetting: Julie Cochrane, in Minion 12 pt on 16
Cover Art & Design: Branko Bistrovic
Paper: Ancient Forest Friendly "Silva" (FSC) — 100% post-consumer waste, totally chlorine-free and acid-free

Ronsdale Press wishes to thank the following for their support of its publishing program: the Canada Council for the Arts, the Government of Canada through the Canada Book Fund, the British Columbia Arts Council, and the Province of British Columbia through the British Columbia Book Publishing Tax Credit program.

Library and Archives Canada Cataloguing in Publication

Bowman, Patrick, 1962–
   Torn from Troy / Patrick Bowman.

(Odyssey of a slave; v. 1)
ISBN 978-1-55380-110-8

   1. Trojan War—Juvenile fiction. I. Title.
II. Series: Bowman, Patrick, 1962– . Odyssey of a slave; v. 1.

PS8603.O97667T67 2011   jC813'.6   C2010-907529-3

At Ronsdale Press we are committed to protecting the environment. To this end we are working with Canopy (formerly Markets Initiative) and printers to phase out our use of paper produced from ancient forests. This book is one step towards that goal.

Printed in Canada by Marquis Printing, Quebec

To my two most steadfast supporters,
the most marvellous daughters
a father could have,

Kathleen and Anitra

ACKNOWLEDGEMENTS

The names of the many people who offered advice on the early versions of this book must go unmentioned here for space reasons. But you know who you are, and I thank you. I would like to single out for special thanks a number of individuals: my sister, Laurel Bowman, for her expert guidance on ancient Greek history and culture, as well as her laser-like ability to identify why my characters kept behaving as they did, and how to stop them; my indefatigable publisher, Ronald Hatch, for wading through multiple drafts with calm professionalism; and my wife, Barbara Cox, for her constant support and for not once complaining about the deteriorating state of the house for well over a year while I wrote this book.

Chapter 1

"ALEXI, WAKE UP!" My sister was leaning over me, her lanky frame silhouetted by the moonlight streaming in the window. Yesterday's celebration had run long into the night, and I mumbled something and rolled over sleepily, face down on the pine planks.

Melantha shook me again. "I mean it! Listen—something's wrong!"

Blinking stupidly, I tried to make sense of the noises from our narrow window. Sandals scuttering up the alleyway. Farther away, urgent shouts of command. And in the distance, screams.

I got to my feet and leaned out. People were running up

the laneway below, the fear in their faces clear in the moonlight. The blacksmith's wife was dragging her two boys by their wrists, not looking back. A few paces behind, old Phylion the potter was hobbling along in his nightshirt and bare feet, cane tapping urgently against the cobbles. The warm night air was heavy with smoke, and from the direction of the city gates came a red glow and the bronze clash of what sounded like weapons.

I called down to the blacksmith's wife. "Ascania! What's going on?"

She didn't look up. Her two boys were crying and trying to turn back as she dragged them grimly up the lane. An uneasy feeling stirred in my stomach.

From nearby came a splintering crash. We craned our heads out farther. At the entrance to Pylacon's smithy a few doors down, I could just make out the shapes of men in armour, torches flickering yellow in their hands. Melantha gasped and wrenched me away from the window. "Lex! Get down! Those are soldiers!"

"Guards? So—"

She shook her head. "Not city guards. Alexi, those are Greeks!"

"Greeks?" I frowned at her. "The Greeks have gone, remember? Besides, how would they get over the wall? Fly?" High as an oak and wide enough for two chariots to race along the top, the city wall had protected us from the barbarians beyond it for as long as I could remember.

"You know who it is? Just some guardsmen, coming home drunk after the party." The Ilian Guard were notorious. I yawned and lay back down on the rough woollen blanket we shared. But as I twisted around, trying to get comfortable, I caught the hollow crunch of wood splintering nearby and a woman's scream, very close. Mela ran to the door and peered out for a moment, then turned to me, her eyes white in the darkness. "Alexi, it's Greeks. I can see them coming up the alley. We have to get out!"

Another door splintered, closer, and there came a harsh, commanding voice. "Every doorway, every building! I don't want a Trojan squadron coming up our backsides because one of you *troglos* missed a house! Now, move! Move!"

I sat up. That was no drunken guardsman. He was speaking Greek! Sweat started from my brow.

"It's too late. They're right across the lane," Mela whispered frantically. "They're checking everywhere. They'll be up here in a moment. Alexi, we need to hide!"

I shook off my panic and peered around the darkened room. Three years of poverty had forced us to sell nearly everything we owned, leaving only a small corner table and stool beside the battered tripod and pot we ate from. Nothing to hide us. I glanced at the window but could hear soldiers right below.

As my hand brushed our tattered blanket, I had an idea. Rolling off it, I darted into the corner behind the door and pulled the blanket over my head.

"Mela! Under here!" The moonlight from the window didn't reach this far. If we were lucky, they might overlook a shapeless lump in the corner.

Mela gave a quick nod but ran to overturn our tiny table and wrench a leg off the stool. As a clatter of brass-nailed sandals came from the stone staircase outside, she snatched up her small dagger and dashed over to squat beside me.

I tugged the blanket over our heads just as two muscular Greek soldiers burst through our door in full battle armour, exploding into the room like huge bronze bulls, ripping the heavy door from its leather hinges. It smashed down across my bare toes and I clenched my teeth to choke off a scream.

The two soldiers prowled around the room, the brass inlays clanking on their leather-strip skirts. Through a rip in the blanket's coarse weave I could see a smoky tallow torch in the first soldier's hand. They peered around suspiciously by its flickering light, their eyes black pools beneath their bronze helmets. I was too frightened to breathe. We'd all heard the stories of what the Greeks did to their prisoners. Struggling not to cough as the oily smoke caught my throat, I reached over beneath the blanket and clutched Mela's hand. Her fingers gripped mine hard.

The second soldier kicked the broken stool, sending it crashing against the rear wall. "*Kopros*," he cursed, glancing at his companion. "Didn't I say it would be empty? Let's go." He stalked out and clattered noisily back down the steps. The soldier with the torch glared around for a moment before heading for the door. I felt a surge of hope.

Too soon. His foot stamped down hard on the door as he left, crushing my smashed toes further and sending a fresh bolt of agony through my foot. He spun toward us at my gasp, thrusting his smoking torch into our darkened corner.

Melantha didn't hesitate. Throwing off the blanket, she leapt to her feet, leaving me hidden.

"Don't kill me!" she called out, drawing her slender frame up tall and straight. She swept her hair over her shoulder with one hand as the other gestured urgently behind her back for me to stay still. Uncertain, I hesitated.

The soldier stepped back in surprise, his hand leaping toward his knife. His helmet tilted as he looked her up and down in her thin shift, and a noise escaped from deep in his throat. "Hey, Takis!" he called out the door. "You missed something!"

In a single swift motion he reached out and threw her over one armoured shoulder, then set off through our shattered doorway, Melantha dangling across his back. As he carried her out I saw her hand slip into her tunic.

Ignoring the stabbing agony in my foot, I scrambled out from beneath the heavy door to hear a shriek from outside. Halfway down the stairs, my sister was hanging off the soldier's back, bronze dagger in her hand. Blood was spurting from a wound on the back of his thigh, spattering the pale stone with droplets that glistened black in the moonlight.

"Filthy *kuna*!" he shrieked. "I'll kill you!" He dropped his torch, grabbing her with both hands to hoist her above his head. She snatched at him but he shook her off easily, his helmet tearing free of its strap and clattering down the steps.

As I started down toward them, the dagger in her flailing hand slashed across the side of his neck, opening a long dark gash. Bellowing with rage, he flung her down the steps. I watched in horror as she tumbled down to smash against the stone well at the bottom. There was a crack like a branch snapping and her scream was abruptly cut off.

Chapter 2

"MELA!" I BLURTED. The soldier's head whipped around, sudden blood spraying from the slash across his neck. Clapping a hand to the wound, he looked up and spotted me in the doorway. He opened his mouth to shout, but nothing came out. His deep-set eyes rolled up into his head and he toppled slowly off the side of the narrow steps to strike the cobbled street below with an armoured crash.

Several Greeks darted out from a side street. "Someone get a healer! Brill's been sheathed!"

Praying for some sign of life, I peered down at my sister's body, dimly lit by the soldier's torch flickering on the ground nearby. She lay still, her head cocked at a harsh angle against the carved well face. The soldier sprawled motionless on the nearby cobbles, his greasy black beard glistening in the light of the torch of the Greek bending over him. I ducked back inside as the man glanced up and barked, "Someone's up there! Dek and Takis, check it out!"

As I reached the centre of our room, my feet slowed. "Mela?" I whispered.

This couldn't be real. Only moments ago we'd both been asleep in the corner. If I could just turn my head, surely she'd still be there, curled up under our blanket. But I couldn't make my head move, afraid of what I wouldn't see.

Some part of me could hear sandals running toward the steps, but I stayed where I was, staring at the far wall. What did it matter now? Near the wall was the stool that Mela had overturned, its leg lying nearby. It had almost fooled them. And when that failed, she'd given herself up. To protect me.

A screech of pain and some hurried footsteps from outside broke into my thoughts. I frowned. What would the gods say of someone who dishonoured a sacrifice like hers? What would Mela say, when we met again in the underworld?

Sandals clumped up the stairs and I looked over at our window.

The laneway below was swarming with Greek soldiers, glittering like armoured beetles in the moonlight. Above the window, unfinished roof beams jutted out from the wall over the street. The men below were looking elsewhere. As the soldiers tramped up the back steps, I scrambled onto the window ledge and leaned out. Ignoring splinters from the rough-hewn beam, I reached up to wrap my hands around it, swinging myself up across the protruding timbers.

Before I could roll out of sight, a soldier's head poked out below me, so close that I could smell his pungent sweat. A dent on his helmet glinted in the moonlight as he turned his head back and forth, scanning the alley below. A bead of sweat dripped from my nose to splash silently on his horse-hair crest. He didn't react. I began to creep silently off the beams and onto the roof.

At that moment the moon came out from behind a cloud. The soldier glanced up and grabbed for me with a shout, but his armoured shoulders were caught in the narrow window. Pulling back with a curse, he thrust out one arm and stabbed blindly at me with a short sword. The blade snagged my tattered *chiton* as I rolled frantically off the beams and onto the flat roof.

I leapt to my feet and teetered across the clattering roof tiles to Glaukon the weaver's at the end of the row, wincing at the agony in my foot. It felt like at least two of my toes were broken. Ahead of me, a wooden bracing beam spanned the street between Glaukon's and the carpenter's workshop across the alley. Praying that the Greeks down the street wouldn't notice, I edged carefully across it, then clambered down to street level along a woody grapevine growing against the workshop wall.

Panting heavily, I leaned against the house wall for a moment, cooling my cheek against the cut stone. Sprawled on the road nearby were two soldiers. Around them, pools of blood shone a dark silver in the moonlight. One was Greek; the other wore the armour of the palace guards. I grimaced. At least he'd taken a barbarian with him. I wondered if their shades were still fighting in Hades.

A soldier at a window spotted me and shouted. Armoured sandals clattered in the street nearby. Despairing, I pushed off from the wall and limped down Kymera Lane. Gods, would they never give up? I ducked inside the shattered door of the Pylacon smithy. A shaft of moonlight lanced the gloom to reveal the clay forge smashed on the hard earth floor. Blacksmithing tools were strewn nearby, and a crumpled form sprawled on a patch of stained earth in the corner. I looked away hastily and hobbled out the back to the packed dirt of Crutch Lane.

As I turned the corner, a crash came from behind me. Two Greeks were stumbling out of the darkness of the smithy. A sewage culvert ran beneath the roadway nearby, and as I limped across it, I had an idea. Trying not to gag, I splashed down into the muck and wormed in feet-first. Hairy creatures brushed past my bare ankles as I disturbed some of Troy's legions of hungry rats. A short way under the road my feet hit some collapsed bricks and I could slide no farther. Plastering some muck over my head, I turned my face to the side, hoping my black hair would be invisible at night. For once, being short for my age was an advantage.

Feet pounded past me, crossing the ditch and continuing toward Brass Pin Lane. Despite the stench, I began to breathe again. Why were they so eager to catch an orphan, anyway? I shuddered, wondering what I'd done.

The footsteps returned. "Hey! Where'd he go?" came a quick, nervous voice. Greek wasn't my native language, but even I could tell he spoke with an accent. "He was straight ahead of us!" Their footsteps stopped above me. "What are we going to tell Ury?"

"Ury can skewer and roast himself," grunted a lower-pitched voice. There was a sniff and the first soldier spoke again. "By the Name! What's that smell?"

"Your hairy armpits," the second one grumbled. "Let's go. We've wasted enough time on this."

Directly above me, the first man spoke again. "Wait a moment. There's a ditch here. You know, I think it goes under the road. Bring that torch over, would you?"

Oh, gods. The terrified whimper in my throat was about to escape. I clamped my lips shut and struggled to slide farther in, but my feet were wedged hard, my broken toes throbbing painfully.

The low voice was speaking again. "You want to go crawling around down there? Suit yourself. It might clean you up a bit."

"Look who's talking, *kopros*-breath! You know that's what they call you, don't you?" The second speaker swore, and there was a clash of armoured bodies wrestling just above me amid muffled curses. I lay motionless, certain they would hear my heart pounding. Something hairy took an experimental nibble at a toe but I didn't breathe.

"Ah, forget it," came the second voice, panting. "He's gone. Let's get back. Those *suagroi* are picking the city clean while we're off chasing some brat. If Ury wants him so badly, let Ury hunt for him." I heard them get to their feet and brush themselves off. As their sandals went back up the road, I caught the nervous voice again. "But you know, we have to decide what we're going to tell Ury. . ." Their voices faded as they turned the corner.

For a long while I lay still, listening for their return. But there was nothing. From the direction of the palace I could still hear the clash and scream of battle.

In the air, overlying the pungent sewage, the sharp tang of smoke recalled my father's description of Greek siege tactics. "If they ever take Troy, they'll be merciless. They'll kill any man or boy of an age to fight, enslave the women, and burn the rest to the ground." On the wind, the smoke of a burning city was fulfilling my father's prophecy.

Chapter 3

I LAY EXHAUSTED in the ditch, my foot throbbing. A swarm of thoughts buzzed through my mind: the Greeks in Troy; the siege of the city; and most of all—Melantha. I bit my lip.

After our father left us three years ago, Melantha had tried to fill the gap. At nineteen, she was four years older, and should have been married long ago. But ten years of war had killed off a lot of potential husbands, and none of those left felt like courting a penniless orphan. Especially as she had insisted to the few who'd asked that I was part of the deal.

She had to be dead. I had heard that same crack watching the butcher up in Temple Street on market day. He was a huge, ruddy man who slaughtered goats by snapping their necks with his thick hands. "Less mess on the vest, eh?" he'd say, flapping his bloody apron and winking at me, then roar with laughter. Later, when meat became scarce and soldiers scarcer, they'd drafted him into a heavy infantry brigade. But the armoury had no breastplates that big, and he went into battle in stiff leather plate. He died two agonizing weeks after stopping a Greek arrow on the Scamander plain.

At least Mela's death had been quick. Was it true what the old women said, that a corpse buried without a gift for the ferryman under the tongue could never rest? Gods, I hoped not.

Maybe she wasn't really dead. That snap could have been something else. Perhaps she hadn't moved because she was unconscious. But then I thought of her head at that unnatural angle, and the horrible crack as she landed. If only I'd listened to her. Or if I'd just kept quiet.

I tried to force my thoughts to something else. For ten years, the wall had kept the Greeks out. The mortar was said to be mixed with ichor from the veins of immortal Poseidon himself. But yesterday, all that had come to an end. How could the Greeks have breached the wall? I frowned, thinking back to the day before.

That morning we had awakened to unfamiliar noises from the street. Rubbing my eyes, I'd sat up from our shared blanket. Melantha was stirring beside me, while the pang in my stomach reminded me that we'd found no supper again the night before. Tying my loincloth tighter, I kicked out the pot shard that wedged our door shut and lifted the edge to swing it open.

Mela and I were late sleepers, and I winced at the bright morning sunlight flooding through the doorway. The noise was coming from the King's Way, the broad boulevard that wound up the hill to the palace, so I stumbled down the steps and headed over.

Mela caught up with me and tossed me the ragged *chiton* that had been my father's. "You want people to think you're a slave?"

Most people wouldn't wear the clothes of the dead, fearing ill fortune, but Mela and I weren't most people. I shrugged and wrapped it on.

At the corner, we stopped short. Hundreds of people were dancing on the broad brick avenue, patrician women in colourful formal *himations* mingling unabashed with beggars in rags. Dancing and singing. It looked like the gods had sent a plague of madness.

Nearby we saw old Alcoa, the half-blind tailor from two streets up, his nightshirt flapping around his bare, spindly legs as he danced past with the well-padded widow from the fishmonger's stall. That was unusual: men and women didn't normally dance together. But that day I saw a lot of rules being broken. I grabbed at his nightshirt as he careened past. "What's going on?"

"Don't you know, boy?" he replied, grinning so widely his wooden teeth were nearly falling out of his mouth. "The barbarians are gone! Packed up and left, by all the gods. Their ships are gone, their camp burned, the war is over! We've beaten them, the filthy *k*—" he spotted my sister and changed course "—uh, crab eaters!" He grabbed at the fish lady and they swirled off, his spindly legs kicking wildly in all directions.

Mela glanced at me, her eyes widening. "Lex! You don't think . . ."

I just looked at her. "Oh, please. Remember when they said the gods had struck all the Greeks blind in the night? This is just another stupid rumour."

She tugged at my hand. "In that case it should be easy to disprove. Or did you have plans?"

Scrounging some breakfast, I was about to say, but she was already weaving through the dancing crowd. I scowled and headed off after her.

Every boy in the city knew the details of the Greek camp. We used to run to the wall whenever we saw a priest sacrificing a goat in front of the temple of Athene, waiting for her wrath to strike the barbarian encampment. The priests kept telling us it would, if we sacrificed enough. Although we watched eagerly for days, it never did. But the priests, who only burned the heart and liver in the sacrifice, always looked well-fed.

So as I climbed the rickety ladder to the archers' ledge

behind the wall, I knew exactly what I'd see: an armada of slender black ships drawn up on the distant beach, surrounded by a forest of stubby grey tents, greasy cooking fires, and a swarm of Greek soldiers. I reached the ledge and looked out over the wide grey top—and stared in disbelief.

"It's true," Mela breathed, clambering up beside me. The grey sailcloth tents and long black ships of the Greeks were gone. Vanished, as if Poseidon's hand had swept the beach clean. I stared, wondering if we'd somehow come to the wrong spot. But there was no mistake: I could still see the deep ruts on the beach where their ships had sat for so long that they'd sunk deep into the sand.

For a moment I felt disoriented. The beach had been covered with ships ever since I could remember, stretching away down the coast. Now, in a single day, every one of them had left, the campfires abandoned, a few tents and stockade walls still smouldering. Even the sharp wooden pikes at the edge of the camp had been knocked down, the wind-dried heads of the Trojan warriors topping them pitched face down in the sand.

Mela and I stood on the archers' ledge for several minutes, staring out at the empty beach. A few other street kids—the war had made a lot of orphans—joined us. Ten years of war couldn't really be over just like that. Could it? I shivered. I hated the war for what it had done to my family, hated the Greek barbarians who had started it, even though I was part Greek myself. But like the bracing beams the stonemasons used, the war had always been there, giving some structure to my life. That, and Mela. I glanced over.

The sea wind above the wall was whipping her long dark hair against her cheek. Most mornings she bound it up with a clasp, but today we'd both dashed out without a thought. Her dark eyes narrowed against the wind as she pulled a fold of her threadbare *himation* back onto her shoulder. It had been our grandmother's, once richly woven and embroidered in red thread with a scene of Artemis hunting, now so faded that the scene was almost invisible. But like my father's *chiton*, it was all she had left to wear.

Eventually, the sounds of revelry drew our attention back to ground level. As I turned to climb down, I spotted the city gates hanging open. That was odd. The large gates were never left open, except for sorties. But nobody was going out; in fact, the soldiers were struggling to drag something in with ropes. Something heavy, by the way they were straining. I craned my head to see, but one of the huge gates blocked my view.

Just then Mela's voice reached me from the foot of the wall. "Alexi! Let's go—there's food!"

I sniffed the air and scrambled back down the ladder, the gates forgotten.

When we returned to our neighbourhood, it looked like the whole city was dancing and drinking on the broad cobbles. I was amazed. Three years of poverty had accustomed us to scraps and an occasional scrawny seagull that I brought down with a well-aimed stone. Now, delicious scents were all around us. Plates of curly dried squid and dark olives in brine, nearly fresh. Dried figs, plates of grapes, even some of the spicy goat meat strips we used to get as a treat. And wine! Not cut ten to one with water the way civilized people took it, but pure, like the drunkards and barbarians did.

Dodging a spray of honey dates thrown to the crowd from a second floor window, I nearly ran into old Sifla, the arthritic crone who worked the bakery we lived above. She scowled as I passed. "Miserable hoarders," she was muttering, her bad eye wandering uncontrollably as she sucked on a date. "Where was all this when we needed it? And me living off lizards and goats' eyes these last three years too."

All the same, oiled by hoarded wine, the giddy mood was catching. Even my sister warmed up, and for the first time in a long while, she had a real smile on her face. She was dancing with the carter's son, a muscular, oiled young man who wore his tunic wrapped much too tight around his broad shoulders. Rumour was that whenever the press gangs grabbed him for service, his mother, an attractive, slightly plump woman with a knowing eye, went to see Prince Hector and persuaded him to let her son go again.

I was just finishing off a few dried figs when my friend Spiros tugged at my arm. "Look, Alexi. Crazy Cassie's out again!"

I looked up. Cassie escaped from the castle regularly, but she'd never come down into our neighbourhood before.

The gods alone knew why she thought she had the gift of prophecy. Most wandering crazies got garbage pitched at them, but since she was King Priam's daughter, people were just pretending they hadn't seen her. Two palace guards trailed uncertainly in her wake.

"Hey, Alexi," Spiros said. "Remember when she said the Greeks were going to attack at the east wall with giant ladders? Zeus, what a squirrel." He snatched a bunch of dark grapes off a passing tray and sucked one into his mouth.

I mounted a crumbling stone step fronting a burnt-out finecloth shop to watch. The shopkeeper had stepped off the wall one night a few years ago, after his son caught an arrow in battle. Come to think of it, the Greeks had attacked along the east wall not long afterwards. But that was stupid. Cassie was always wrong, it was probably the only thing everyone in Troy agreed on. That, and how filthy the Greeks were.

Her beautifully embroidered *himation* of glowing green was never meant for our part of town. It dragged on the oily cobblestones behind her as she drifted up the alley toward us, running her fingertips over anything in reach. I watched her stoop to brush her fingers over a broken doll in the gutter before reaching out to touch a young woman's face, shaking her head sadly.

Despite the crowds, people were carefully opening a path as she walked. Stepping up beside me as she approached, Spiros spat a seed into the gutter. "Zeus, she's slipped right off the anvil today!"

In spite of her hollow-eyed stare, she was stunning. Dark, wavy hair flowed over perfect cheekbones to drape across her bare shoulders. Captivated, I didn't look down fast enough. She looked my way and her eyes widened. Before I could step down, she had come up beside me to grab my shoulders, peering intensely into my face. Quicker than me, Spiros had vanished into the crowd.

"All . . . dead." She was speaking only to me, her scented breath hot in my face. Gods. She was just my height, her full lips only a finger's length from mine. I found myself wondering what would happen if I leaned forward and kissed them.

Wait—what was she saying? "The city of Priam, aflame and dying." Her voice was oddly flat, speaking of things she'd already seen. "The wasps burst from the swollen hive." Her voice grew louder. "Stinging, burning. Dark silver in the streets. Temples defiled." Her eyes had drifted, but swivelled back to lock onto mine. "Nobody believes. But you—" she stared hard for a moment. "Live. Accept your father's gift."

Easy to see why King Priam was having trouble getting her married off. But she wasn't done yet. Her eyes widened suddenly and her voice rose to a shriek, her fingers tightening on my shoulders. "I see it! I see them now! Soldiers inside it! Beneath the moon, they spill out . . . sweet Hera believe me! Oh, gods—" she broke off and began to convulse, eyes rolling up into her head. I shook myself at the sight. Kiss *that*? If I wanted a quick and painful death, maybe. I twisted away but her sharp fingers clung to my shoulders with a mad strength, and she was tugged off balance as I pulled away.

Her foot slipped on the greasy step and she pitched forward. There was a wet crunch from behind me as I slid sideways into the crowd. I should have kept going, but I turned back to watch, peering out from behind a fattish man with a basket of bread.

She was lying on the ground, blood welling from a gash in the side of her temple where it had struck the step. One of the guards was on his feet, sword waving anxiously as the other knelt beside her, trying to stem the flow with his filthy fingertips. Stupid *koprophages*. Didn't they know anything about healing?

I couldn't resist. "Nice guarding, crabs!" I called from behind the basket. There were a few chuckles around me. Their carefully polished armour and the rumour that they scuttled sideways from danger had earned the palace guards that nickname.

But not to their faces. The fattish man glared down at me and moved pointedly away as the guard's gaze snapped in our direction. Shoving the fat man aside, he stepped forward and grabbed me under the arm, yanking me out of the crowd hard enough to dislocate something. His fist was already up when a soft voice drifted up from the cobbles.

"Stop. Bring him." Her voice was weak. "He will heal me." My head jerked around, startled. Me?

The guard turned to stare at her for a moment, then

shrugged. "You heard her highness," he grunted, throwing me to the ground at her feet. "Start healing." His sword dug pointedly into the back of my neck as the other guard scuttled out of the way.

Heal her? What was she talking about? I'd helped my father in his surgery a few times, but this was serious. The way the blood was gushing from her head, in a few minutes all she'd need would be a shroud. I dithered, trying to think of what to do.

A growl from behind and a painful prod in my back urged me on. Right. What would my father have done? Um—stop the bleeding, I guessed. I pressed down with the heel of one hand across the wound, slowing the gush to a trickle between my fingers. So far, so good. I vaguely remembered my father saying how the gods respected cleanliness in healers, and glanced around the garbage-strewn alleyway. Let's hope they'd overlook it this time. Now, what would my father have done next? Bandage the wound. Yes. I shouted over my shoulder. "Cloth strips! I need cloth strips! Now!"

Behind me, I could hear ripping cloth and a shriek of dismay as some citizen was volunteered to give up part of her tunic. A moment later a few strips of fine linen dropped on the back of my head. Maybe there was something to be said for the crabs after all. I reached up with my free hand and grabbed one, then—*kopros*. This was going to take both hands. As I took my other hand away to fold the strip into a pad, her head started gushing blood again. I slapped the pad into place frantically and began my father's slow chant to Apollo, god of healing.

It took three full chants before the blood stopped seeping. As with so many of the gifts from the gods, nobody knew why they had filled us with blood, but people never did well without it. Cassie had drifted in and out of consciousness as I was treating her, and now as I bound up the gash with a tight fresh cloth, her green eyes flickered open and those full lips of hers smiled. "I knew you'd do that," she murmured, satisfied. "Remember your father's gift."

Spiros punched my shoulder as we trotted off. "Hey Lex— I think she likes you!"

Could he tell what I'd been thinking about her? "Go grope a fig tree, would you? At least the girls talk to me."

It had come out harsher than I meant. Cursed by the gods with a cruelly twisted lip, Spiros wasn't likely to ever land himself a girl without paying her. I tried to change the topic. "What Cassie was saying—did it make any sense to you? Wasps? Defiled temples?"

He shrugged. "How should I know? War's made a lot of people crazy." Throwing the rest of his handful of grapes into the gutter, he loped off. It was the last time I saw him alive.

At the time, I had just shrugged. Someone was piping a tune on a pan flute nearby, and several girls were dancing in a circle by the polished stone steps of the temple of

Hestia. One of them, a dark-eyed girl from down by the fish market, glanced at me out of the corner of her eye as I watched her. I wish I'd had the nerve to ask her to dance.

As the evening drifted into a warm night, people started staggering home, drunk and exhausted. Finally, I picked my own way back, stepping over revellers who had passed out in the streets. The pure wine had destroyed my balance, and I nearly tumbled over the wall of the ornate carved well at the foot of our steps. The well had been dug years ago when the lower town was still fashionable. The gentry had moved uphill after it went dry, leaving behind a decaying corner of the city.

Stepping carefully around the well, I lurched up the outside stairway to the room that Mela and I shared. It was just a storage room over the bakery, but after her husband died old Sifla couldn't make it up the stairs so she let us stay there. Mela wasn't home yet, and I collapsed onto our shared blanket on the floor to drop off quickly.

It had been later the same night that I was awakened by the sounds of Greek invaders putting Troy to the torch.

Chapter 4

I HUDDLED IN the culvert beneath the roadway all night, despair washing over me in slow waves. For the first time in my life, I felt completely alone.

When I was younger, my father had always been around. Later in the war, when he became too busy to come home much, he'd brought me with him to his *xeneon* to watch and, later, to help treat his patients. With his deep, rumbling voice and his power of life, I used to imagine that he was the god Zeus himself, come to earth.

Unlike Zeus, my father was always patient. And unlike those healers who, proud of their reputations, shunned cases they couldn't help, my father never turned anyone away, even those about to die. "Just remember, Alexi," he had murmured to me once, "if you can't cure them, you can still relieve their pain."

After he'd left us, Mela had stepped in—preparing meals, helping with my lessons and, later, scrounging with me for food.

Above me, the sounds of battle had died down, and the few soldiers who came clanking down the road were Greek. I could hear them laughing and talking to one another, not bothering to lower their voices. I could only guess what that meant. Eventually fatigue overcame fear, and I drifted off, to unpleasant dreams.

I slept fitfully in the culvert until early morning when a noise woke me. A ragged column of women and children were coming down the lane. A few wore fine embroidered *himatia*, mostly torn and stained; others had on nightshirts or were completely naked. But they all walked with their heads down and shoulders slumped, hands in front of them, their feet barely clearing the ground. There were no men among them.

In their midst was the dark-eyed girl I'd seen dancing at the temple. Had it been just yesterday? I opened my mouth to call, but something stopped me. Her head was downcast, her torn tunic half off her shoulder and stained with blood. Her dulled eyes looked my way, but her gaze slid right past me. It was then that I spotted the leather thongs binding her wrists.

As the last of them passed by my hiding spot, several Greek soldiers followed, laughing, long spears on their armoured shoulders, helmets under their arms. One of them lifted his spear to jab at an aging woman lagging behind the others. It was old Sifla. She staggered and nearly fell, but the others didn't even lift their heads. She caught her balance and scrambled to catch up. Helpless, I closed my eyes, and the procession trudged off down the road toward the city gates.

When the shuffling footsteps had died away, I struggled warily out of the culvert. After the noise and terror of the previous night, the city was eerily silent under a flat grey sky. The battle sounds were gone, but the smell of smoke lingered on the chill morning breeze like the remains of some vast burnt offering.

Thirst and a desperate need to rinse off the sewer muck turned me toward a well nearby in Brass Pin Lane. My foot had stiffened up during the night, leaving me hobbling. Several times I had to duck into doorways to hide from Greek soldiers, but it was easier today. Last night they were invaders, swords out and alert for danger; this morning, they swaggered past with the easy confidence of conquerors. I wondered again how the city could have fallen so swiftly.

I passed a dozen dead bodies, mostly soldiers slumped against walls where they'd backed up until they could retreat no further. Almost all were Trojan, armour already looted, their deep, savage gashes the work of the Greeks' short swords. It wasn't until I turned the narrow corner at Clutch Way that I stumbled across someone I knew.

It was Spiros. A pool of dark blood stained the cobbles behind his head, matting his hair. I looked for some sign of struggle, proof that he'd fought back, but his wide-open eyes just stared up at me with what might have been surprise. One of the few stray curs that hadn't been caught and eaten was sniffing around tentatively. I threw a stone to chase it away, catching its bony flank, but it just trotted off a few steps before sitting down to wait, tongue lolling.

In a doorway nearby I found a brightly painted pot shard and slipped it under my friend's tongue. His lips were cold and rubbery to the touch. There was nothing else I could do for him now, and I moved on. The dog watched me go.

The well was in the middle of the square where Brass Pin Lane met Hog Run, and I watched from the shadows for a little while before approaching. The grey stone shops around the square had the usual sprinkling of ochre graffiti that had sprung up since the last rain. Pictures of Greek soldiers dying under Trojan chariots competed for space with angular naked women and a risky picture of King Priam and a goat. I wondered who had drawn it. Not that it mattered. If old Priam was still alive, he had more important things on his mind.

The square was empty. I limped to the well and had drawn several buckets when I heard voices. Dropping the bucket back into the well, I hobbled for the opposite side of the square, wincing.

Just off the corner was a spot where there had once been

a narrow lane between two buildings. Carpenter Halitos, the crotchety owner on one side, had built a wall across it to keep us from cutting through into Dog Leg Alley. But he was no mason, and the badly-fitted stones had left a dozen footholds, making it a popular spot to spy on the girls drawing water at the well. I scrambled over it, smudging an ochre drawing of a Greek warrior with a rounded butt for a face, then turned to peer out between the gaps at the top.

The soldiers appeared around the corner. Greeks, naturally. I hadn't seen a living Trojan man since yesterday. There were three of them, heading for the well.

One of them pointed at the ground with a shout, and I realized with a shock that my wet footprints on the cobbles led directly toward me. As they started heading my way, I dropped to the ground and hobbled off down Bent Ox Lane, rounded the corner—and ran straight into a group of Greek soldiers looting a bronzework shop.

Chapter 5

THE SOLDIERS REACTED instantly. One of them grabbed me by the shoulders and Expertly kicked my legs out from under me, dropping me face-down onto the cobbles. A knee crushed into my back, driving my breath out in a gasp as fingers grabbed my hair to yank my head up, a sharp point digging painfully into the side of my throat. From behind my head came a garlic-tainted Greek voice. "Got another one, Lopex. Too old to train. I'll trench him here."

A surge of anger overwhelmed me. "Pretty brave of you, killing a boy," I snapped. Thinking about the soldiers last night, I added, "Gods, you stink. What do you scrub with, dead rats?"

There was a coarse laugh from a few soldiers nearby and

the man on my back cursed. My head was wrenched up to expose my throat. I braced myself.

But what came instead was a voice. "Hold, Ury." A pair of battle-worn sandals stopped in front of my face. "Turn him."

The knee was lifted from my back and I was roughly rolled over. Two Greeks were looking down at me. The man pinning me down was hairy and unkempt, with dark, angry eyes and a bushy black beard that didn't look like it had ever seen a comb. I had an instant to wonder why those deep eyes looked familiar before the other man spoke, his face upside down to mine.

"Where'd you learn the hero's tongue, boy?"

I realized I'd spoken in Greek. "What's it to you?"

He looked at me for a moment. "Nothing. But it might keep you alive. Now answer." His companion banged my head on the cobbles for emphasis.

I scowled. "My grandmother. She was Greek."

"That could be useful. How old are you?"

"Twelve." I was fifteen, but recalling my father's warning, knocked off a few years. Once again, I was glad to be small for my age.

His gaze lingered on my hair for a moment. Straight and black like Mela's, it was almost as unusual as our grey eyes. Finally, he nodded. "You'll do. Feel like being useful, Trojan?"

"Lopex, you heard what the little filth said to me," the angry-eyed man growled. "He'll be trouble. I say trench him now."

The other man spoke, his voice low and even. "I heard him, Ury. His mind is quick, and his Greek is good." He knelt down beside my head. "Your choice, boy. Decide now."

The thought of helping these butchers made me sick. An angry retort was rising to my lips when I caught a glint of sunlight off Ury's dagger as he shifted his grip. Self-preservation broke through for a heartbeat, and I looked up at the shorter man and nodded.

Ury grunted angrily.

"I've decided, Ury. But if he doesn't work out, you can have him." The second man turned away to supervise the men looting the shop.

"Right, then," Ury said, turning back to me with a disappointed scowl. "You heard him. Lopex owns you now. You do what he says. *Whatever* he says. And if you ever even raise a finger against a free man, you'll be dead before your next breath. Got that, boy?"

I nodded. He grabbed me by the hair and slammed my head against the cobbles again. "What was that?"

"I got that," I muttered. "*Sir.*"

"That's right you do. When a free man speaks to you, you answer. Now tell me your name, boy."

"Alexias. I mean, Alexias, *sir.*" I corrected myself, hating it.

He put his lips down beside my ear. "If you *ever* speak to me again like you just did now, you little *skatophage*, I'll cut out your tongue before you can take another step." He smashed my head on the ground once again and hauled me to my feet by my hair. "Right, Lopex," he called. "Your Trojan filth is ready."

The other man walked over, and I got a better look at him. He didn't look that tall, slightly shorter than the hulking soldiers around him. His dark, pointed beard, shot through with flecks of silver, was well combed and trimmed close to a hard jaw. Despite his stature, he had broad, powerful shoulders outlined beneath a worn but finely woven *chiton*, and thick, hairy legs, slightly bowed. He reminded me a little of a monkey I'd once seen on a sailor's shoulder. Except for his eyes. Their proud gaze openly dared the world to hand him something that he couldn't hand back in knots.

He looked me over for a moment, his arms folded across his chest. "You say your grandmother was Greek, boy?"

I took a deep breath. "Yes," I said, gritting my teeth as I added, "master." He continued to look at me until I added, "Elena of Patras."

He glanced away as one of his men came and spoke to him, gesturing back at the cart now creaking under a load of polished brass plate. "Well, boy, your first task is to find a route through the city to the main gate, one we can bring this cart through. And boy?" he added as an afterthought, picking up a large bow and slinging it across his shoulder. "Stay close. Don't look like you're trying to escape." One of his men gave a guttural laugh.

I looked at the cart. "What, that?" I broke off at his expressionless glance and began again. "I mean, um, master, with that cart the quickest way is up Hog Run to Temple Street, then down King's Way to the gate." He gestured at me to lead, and I started back out the alley.

Behind me, the cart began to rattle over the cobblestones. I glanced back. He had two men pulling it by its shafts and three more pushing. It would be easy to escape; I knew the city, and they hadn't even tied my hands. I wondered why not.

I kept my eye open for a chance to bolt, but we were going too slowly. Every few paces we had to stop to drag bodies out of the way of the wheel. Many of the bodies were men in bits of Trojan armour, their gaping wounds a sign that they'd died in battle. At least as many, mostly older men, wore the clothes they'd had on for the festival. Some had been cut down as they ran or backed against a wall and executed, but many still lay where they'd passed out in the street after last night's party, stabbed in their sleep.

As I rounded the last sharp corner leading into King Priam Square, a noise caught my ear. A short distance ahead, a member of the city's elite Ilian Guard was kneeling over a body beside the wall, his face in his hands. He looked up at my approach, his cheeks wet, and I shook my head for silence and jerked a thumb behind me toward the Greeks, just emerging into the square. I glanced back to see if they'd noticed him, and when I turned around again, he had vanished.

As I passed the body he had been kneeling at, a sprawling,

curly-haired Trojan soldier with his jaw slashed off, it twitched and heaved to one side. I sprang back as the Ilian guardsman erupted from beneath the corpse. He leapt to his feet and rushed past me, his eyes burning with a manic hatred, spear levelled at the Greeks behind me.

He didn't even get close. An arrow buzzed through the air toward him, sank into his throat—and shot out the back of his neck, landing with a clatter on the cobbles on the far side of the square. Hands clutching his throat, he gurgled blood for a moment, staggered, and collapsed.

Lopex was standing behind the cart, his bow in his hands. I stared, astonished. Maybe the gods could do it, but no mortal I'd ever heard of could shoot an arrow right through a man, even at close range. He hadn't even taken time to aim. His men were grinning openly. I shuddered, thinking about how I'd been planning to run. No one could outrun a bolt from a bow in those hands. He jerked his head for me to continue.

The metallic smell of blood assaulted me as we moved into the square. The worst of last night's fighting must have been here. On the far side, the Scaean gates sagged wide open. Bodies were everywhere, the cobbles underfoot sticky with so much blood that it was still congealing. Meat rotted quickly in this heat, and the square was already alive with the buzz of flies in the afternoon sun. Near the east side of the square was something huge and wooden. I blinked, trying to make it out against the glare. Lying on its side and mostly burnt, what remained looked like part of a giant wooden bull. Or a horse. I shook my head.

The Greeks behind me cursed as they spotted fallen comrades, but Lopex overrode them. "We won't leave them. But first we must get this wagon down to the ship. Would the dead ask us to risk losing the treasure we fought for? We'll prepare a hero's pyre for the fallen once these pickings are safe on board."

It was late afternoon when I passed through the massive wooden gates of Troy. The huge bronze insignia of a lion on one gate glared down at me while the sad-eyed owl on the other watched me leave. They looked undamaged. However the barbarians had gotten in, it hadn't been through here.

A cool gust of wind made me shiver. I'd peered over the wall a thousand times but never been beyond it. I looked back through the gates at the main square, wondering if I'd ever return. But there was nothing to return to any more.

Drawn up on the beach not far away were the Greek ships that had vanished from the sight of the city watchtowers yesterday morning. Wherever they'd gone, it hadn't been far. There must have been over a hundred of them, long and thin, lying like huge black daggers on the stony beach. Many had two oversized white eyes painted on the front and a high, carved tail at the back, curling like a scorpion poised to strike. Large groups of men were camped around the ships, and we passed several looting parties heading back into the city.

When we reached the beach, I was corralled between two ships with some fifty other captives, a small fraction of the number the Greeks must have taken last night. Two girls about my age were huddled together in the shade of a hull, arms around one another, weeping. A three-year-old boy sat nearby, his arms around his knees, rocking back and forth and whimpering. His mother lay motionless beside him, gore leaking down her face from a massive eye wound, flies crawling on her cheeks. But most of the captives simply sat, staring numbly at nothing.

A lone Greek soldier with a bulging lower lip frowned sourly down at us from the deck, fingering a battered bronze spear with his left hand. Folds of sunburnt skin creased into angry lines around his eyes. Sprouting from his right shoulder was a stump instead of an arm, but he could still chase us down if we tried anything. Besides, as a hawk-faced Trojan woman nearby snapped when she saw me eyeing him, "Planning to run? Where are your brains, boy? At least as slaves we'll get fed. The Greeks are stripping the city bare. Anybody left behind when they leave will starve, I shouldn't wonder."

Slaves? The word came as a shock. The thought left me brooding until a scent wafting from a nearby cooking fire caught my attention. The Greeks had driven the palace's scrawny goats out of the city and were systematically slaughtering and cooking them. Seasoned with looted spices, the meat smelled incredible.

Gods, I was hungry. I slipped between the soldiers clustered around the nearest cooking fire and was stretching to reach one of the bronze-tipped skewers when something smashed into my ear, sending me sprawling. I looked up to see a Greek soldier hulking over me. "Get lost, brat," he growled, shaking the skewer at me. "Touch a free man's meal again and I'll kill you before you can taste it."

I sat up, rubbing my ear. "So what am I supposed to eat?" I shot back.

His armoured toe cap smashed into my shin before I could dodge. "Answer me back, will you, slave?" he snarled. I rolled aside before his next kick could connect, and hobbled away. Silhouetted by the cooking fire, the soldier grunted into the darkness after me for a moment before returning to his meal. Resentful, I skulked in the gloom beyond the firelight.

The crowds of Greeks milling around the cooking fires gradually thinned. As the last soldiers finally left the closest one, the hawk-faced woman sitting nearby scrambled up. I stood tentatively to follow her, a painful throbbing in my shin adding to the pain in my head.

"Find somewhere else, boy," she barked, the threads in her gown flashing in the firelight as she spun toward me. "Touch something here and lose a hand."

I stopped in dismay. Were my fellow Trojans against me too? My distress must have shown in my face, because after a moment she pursed her lips and sighed heavily. "Oh, all right, boy. Puny thing like you won't eat much anyway."

Taking my cue from her, I began sifting through the embers. Cooking skewers were hard to control, and a few bits of meat had slipped off them as the Greeks ate, falling into the coals or onto the ground nearby. As we scrounged, she warmed up slightly. She had been the wife of an oil merchant recruited into the Trojan army about three years ago, but he had fallen beneath the wheels of a Greek chariot six months past. When I asked about her children, she snorted and glanced up. I dove for a scrap by her feet.

"Children? Not likely. My Nico never had the stuffing for it. Tried for five years but got nowhere." After a pause, she added, "'Course, I'm glad of it now. Who'd want their children ending up as slaves?"

Gods, I wished she'd stop saying that word. As I chewed on a scrap of gristly meat, the sand gritty against my teeth, an animal howl rose from down the beach.

Ury, the hairy man who had nearly killed me this afternoon, was holding his knuckles against his head, his face contorted in the light of a nearby fire. Before him, two men were carrying a helmetless Greek soldier on a long shield, his limbs dangling. As they set the shield down, the soldier's lifeless head flopped toward me, revealing familiar deep-set eyes and a coarse black beard. I realized with a shock why Ury's face had seemed familiar.

Ury grabbed the smaller man. "Deklah!" he cried, shaking him violently. "What happened? *What happened to my brother?*"

The man was being shaken so hard he couldn't speak, and his sputtering only made Ury angrier. The taller man mumbled something.

"What?" shouted Ury, dropping the first man.

"Ury," the tall man began nervously. "Brill was looting a house. In the alleys on the east side. He was bringing a slave girl out when—" he paused.

"When what?" Ury roared.

"There was someone else in the house." The man hesitated. "He stabbed Brillicos in the neck as he came out the door." I peered at him. He couldn't think *I'd* done that. Could he? I listened harder.

Ury had stepped back to stare at both men. In the flickering firelight, his eyes had an inhuman look. "But you killed him." His voice was quieter. "The man who did this."

The man Ury had called Deklah looked down, rubbing the back of his arm with his other hand. "You know, Ury, it was like this. We tried, but—"

I glanced up. It was the voice of the soldier who had nearly found me in the ditch. Ury's head swivelled to look at him. "But what?" he roared.

Deklah cringed and looked down. "He got away," he muttered.

"A Trojan frog-eater, he got away from you, two armed Greek soldiers?" A vein bulged on Ury's forehead. "What was he? An immortal?"

Deklah's head snapped up. "Yes—that was it! He was

incredibly strong, and he fought like a Fury. An immortal, he must have been."

The tall man jumped in. "We had him cornered on a rooftop, but he jumped right across the street to another. So we chased him down to street level and through the alleys for half the night. But then he just—disappeared."

Deklah nodded vigorously as I held my breath. Surely not even a Greek barbarian could be taken in by a story like that.

"You mean you let my brother's killer go?" Ury shouted.

They both spoke at the same time. "But, Ury—like we said—"

"Do you even know what he looked like? Would you know him again?"

The men glanced at one another. Finally Deklah spoke. "You have to understand, Ury, it was dark. We never saw his face."

Ury's expression contorted again and the men cringed. "Nothing?" he roared. "Is there *nothing* you can tell me about him?"

"Wait, I remember." The taller man spoke up. Now that I was listening for it, I recognized that deep voice as the second man who had been chasing me. "He had a limp."

Ury rounded furiously on him. Behind him, Deklah was frantically shaking his head. "He limped?" roared Ury. "*You couldn't catch a cripple?*"

Deklah broke in anxiously. "No, no. Not like that, not at

all. You know, Ury, it was really a small limp. Hard to spot. And it didn't slow him down, no, not a bit."

Ury looked at them for a long moment. His red face gradually lost its colour, and he walked over to his brother's corpse, lying on the sand. When he spoke again his voice was almost inaudible. "I promise you this, Brillicos—I will find your killer." His hand stroked a leather pouch at his waist. "I will make him beg to die. I promise you this."

I shuddered.

An older, gaunt captive with a slight stoop was standing nearby. I hadn't seen him approach. His short-cropped hair and beard were grey and his face lined, but his gaze was steady and intelligent. He looked away from me as he spoke, watching the moonlit waves crash on the beach.

"Beware of him," he murmured. His voice was quiet and refined, his Trojan bearing a slight accent. "Eurylochos—Ury—is an animal. I've seen what he does to men he's captured. Whoever Ury's looking for, he'd be better off dead than in the hands of that creature."

Chapter 6

"GET UP, YOU LAZY Trojan pigs! You want food, you work for it!"

I opened my eyes and rolled to the side to dodge a wooden spear butt, but it thudded into my side as I scrambled up, knocking me to my knees in the sand and sending a jolt of pain through my leg as my broken toes took the pressure.

"Get down! I didn't tell you to stand up!" the one-armed Greek guard snarled down at me.

"Yes you did! You said—" but the spear butt ground into my throat, choking off my wind.

"Talk back to me, you snot-nosed scum? Next time it's the sharp end. Now stand!"

Around me, the knot of slaves I'd slept among were scrambling warily to their feet. I followed their lead, staying bent over, ready to drop or duck.

"That's better!" He jabbed his spear at us with a foul laugh. "Now, march!" As far as I could tell, none of the other captives spoke Greek, but his meaning was clear.

I was put to work loading the treasure the Greeks had looted. Most of the ships had already been pushed off the beach into the water, and several of us were ordered to carry bundles out to them. The waves rolled up around my feet as I stood on the shore. Thanks to the Greek war, which had started when I was five, I had never before been this close to the sea. I didn't even know how to swim.

"Get going! What are you waiting for, low tide?" A spear butt prodded me in the back and I stumbled forward into the surf. It was a strange feeling, the sea water foaming around my legs. The waves were rough, and twice I staggered and nearly dropped my bundle before I learned to lean into them as they rolled past. By the time I reached the ship they were up to my armpits, forcing me to hold my arms above my head.

On board, several Greek sailors were stowing our bundles below the open benches that stretched across the ship. An enormously fat, one-eared man sat in the shade beneath a sail draped over some oars, grunting commands at the sailors.

Plates, armour, finecloth and jewellery—as I climbed the net up the ship's flank I wondered who they had been stolen from. Not us, of course. In the three years since our father had gone, everything we had owned had been traded for food. When no one was looking I let my bundle sag open, spilling some of their precious stolen jewellery into the surf. Maybe they'd even find it again. In a thousand years, perhaps.

We spent two days loading a river of looted treasure onto the ships. Convoys of Greek soldiers emerged regularly from the gates with wagons laden, a never-ending stream of ants picking over Troy's charred bones. I was kept busy loading from first light to well after dark.

It was on the third morning that a foul smell woke me from an exhausted sleep. The wind had dropped, and the whiff of rotting meat wafting from the city had become a stench strong enough to turn my stomach. I gagged. The Greeks had been so intent on their looting that they hadn't even bothered to bury the bodies that were lying in the streets.

Nearby, our one-armed guard was sitting on a rock, talking to another soldier. He spat into the sand, wrinkling his nose. "Hera's harness, what a stench!" he muttered. "If we're not off this beach by noon heat, won't be a soldier here can keep his guts down."

Knots of strained conversation formed among the Greeks, and after a hasty breakfast they began preparations to sail. Most of the captives, along with the Greek chariots, horses, and the largest stolen statues, were sent to a set of wide, flat-bottomed ships clustered at the far end of the beach. The two girls I'd seen earlier had been torn, weeping, from each other's arms and sent to separate ships. The hawk-nosed woman, the older man and I were all assigned to a long, thin vessel near the centre of the fleet. I hadn't seen the young boy since they'd dragged his mother's lifeless body away to the cess trench.

The ship we'd been sent to was well over forty strides long. At its widest point, a tall man could lie across it with his arms above his head and barely touch both sides. The hull was made of overlapping planks, coated on the outside with black pitch. Molten and runny in the noontime sun, it gave off a sharp pine smell that stung my nostrils as I climbed up the stern ladder, but it was pleasant compared to the stench from the city.

There were four other captives standing on a deck that covered the rear quarter of the boat, two middle-aged women and a couple of frail older men including the one who had spoken to me on the beach. A Greek sailor with a round, weather-beaten face and tufts of dark hair sprouting from his ears stood facing us, arms folded. "Right!" he shouted at us. "You slaves get up to the front double quick, see? Head up under that bow deck and don't come out till you're told."

The others shuffled their feet uncertainly. The sailor grunted in frustration. "Oh, for Athene's sake—don't any of you lot speak Greek?"

"I do," I muttered.

"Oho. You're *that* one, are you? Well, keep that tongue on a leash or you'll lose it, boy. Now send your friends up under the bow deck." He pointed. "But you stay put, do you hear?"

I grunted an explanation, and the other slaves began to pick their way toward the deck that covered the front quarter of the boat. Between the two decks at the front and rear, some twenty or thirty benches stretched across from one side of the boat to the other. They were about three foot-lengths apart, and the shorter women in particular struggled to step between them without falling into the gap. Nobody was telling me to do anything, so I squatted against the railing at the rear of the ship to wait.

A few minutes later, the soldiers started up the ladder to take their seats on the rowing benches. On either side of the rear deck, two older men sat down on small wooden seats, one on either side of the high curved tail. Like Lopex, they had small beards, carefully trimmed to a short point. They took hold of two long, flat-ended poles like oversized oars and trailed them in the water.

As the ship rowed away from the beach, I stood up at the rear wooden rail and looked back. Five other ships were setting off in our wake. Out on the water, the breeze carried away the smells of rotting meat and fresh pitch. On the distant hill behind the beach, the gates of Troy sprawled open, smoke spiralling into the sky from the blackened city they hadn't protected. For the first time since I'd been captured, it occurred to me to wonder where we were going.

Behind me came a raspy cackle. "Missing your mama, boy? Well, don't you worry, I'm sure some Greek soldier is doing right by her just about now."

I turned around. One of the two grizzled men was leaning on his pole, leering at me. I grunted back at him. "My mother died when I was a baby. Probably back when you were only eighty."

He spat on the deck. "You're lucky I'm sitting comfortable here, slave boy, or you'd feel my fist. You feel like dying, you just keep up that backtalk."

I looked down, trying to hide my anger. He must have taken it for submission. He took a swig from his wine skin and went on. "Old Lopex's got plans for you, boy, or you'd be stowed below with the others. Probably ship's boy. If you're good enough, and quick enough, he'll keep you. Otherwise—" he shrugged. "So here's some free learning, from me to you, because we need a ship's boy again. The last one, he didn't work out so good." He took another swig and wiped his mouth on his tunic.

"When they order you up to the bow—that's the front up there—you get up there quick. Ship's boy is no good that can't hop the benches at double speed. Mind you don't foul the oars. And if they points you to the stern, that's back here."

I turned back to watch Troy shrink behind us. A black plume of smoke stained the pale blue sky above it. Behind the boat a dozen gulls circled and shrieked at each other. One dove to catch a fish, and I felt queasy as it disappeared under the waves. Just how far below us was the sea bottom—if there was one? Out here on the water, anything could be lurking beneath us.

My grandmother used to tell me stories from her past of monsters beneath the surface, vast whirling pools that sucked in ships, and strange creatures that waited to strip the flesh from men's bones. They'd terrified me, but she seemed to enjoy them, her hands waving cheerfully as she described the man-eating fish as big as islands, the horrible forms of Poseidon's wrath. In Troy we were landsmen, using ships only for local trade and fishing. But the Greeks, with their long-distance vessels, actually seemed to *like* the sea.

The ship had started to tip back and forth like a rocking chair, interrupting my thoughts, and I had to brace myself to keep from falling. I looked around uneasily, wondering if we were about to sink. But nobody else looked worried. I clung to the rail, hoping it would stop.

"Get used to it, boy," the sailor rasped. "This is mild."

I staggered a bit as I let go of the rail to turn around. "Sure it is," I muttered.

"You just know all about everything, don't you? Well, city boy, you just wait till they put the sail up, or it comes on to blow, then watch. Sometimes she tosses so much that even old Zeus couldn't hold these steering oars steady. Now that's when we've got the most important job on the ship. Ain't that right, Praxy?"

His companion gave a toothless grunt.

"Right," I muttered vaguely. I didn't know if I was more relieved that the rocking was normal or alarmed at the thought of storms. The talkative sailor lapsed into irritated silence.

Facing forward, the men rowing caught my eye. I hated to admit it, but it was an impressive sight. Some fifty men in two rows pulled the boat's long oars in perfectly timed sweeps like a well-practised dance. I sat down against the rail to watch, wondering why they were all facing backward.

Each stroke had two parts: a strong, high pull as they swept the oar handles toward them and a long return as they pushed it back low and flat to prepare for the next stroke. Despite the complex pattern, all fifty oars hit the water with a single splash. Regardless of what we'd been told, these barbarians were superbly trained sailors.

The hypnotic movement of the oars matched the steady tune from the pace keeper's flute. Watching the chariot of Helios creep slowly across the sky reminded me of days in Troy. When we'd found enough to eat, Mela and I used to bask in the sun on the wall, at least until the lookouts chased us off. Mela used to wonder if Helios and Apollo really were the same god, as the monoists said. I choked on the unexpected memory.

Suddenly a voice interrupted the rhythmic creak of the oars. It was the sharp-eyed man, Lopex, waving at me from the deck at the front where he'd been talking to Ury and the hairy-eared sailor. "Boy! Up front! Now!"

I staggered to my feet, trying to keep my balance on the rocking deck while I looked for a way forward. The area below the benches was stuffed with bales and crates of goods stolen from Troy, piled almost up to the underside of the benches; no way through there. Above, I could just about hop from bench to bench, but there was no way past those milling oars.

I watched the oarsmen on the closest bench for a moment. There were two, one pulling an oar on each side. As they pulled, the handles of the oars travelled high and slowly through the air, their tips far apart. But when the oarsmen pushed back for another stroke, the oar handles on each side were low, so close they nearly touched.

"Boy! Are you deaf? Get up here, now!"

I looked around wildly. How could he expect me to get up there through that thicket of churning oars? In desperation, I looked at the nearest two oarsmen again. As the handles came sweeping low toward me, I hopped over them, landing on the bench between the two rowers, careful to favour my bad foot. But now the power stroke was beginning. Fifty oars were rising at once, including the two now behind me. I waited, then leapt to the next bench, turning sideways to fit through the gap between the next set of oars, now at their widest separation. As they caught up with me, I waited for them to reverse and hopped over them on the same bench as they swept past, then leapt to the next.

Leap, pause, turn sideways, leap, step, leap again. I couldn't even look up to see how far I'd come. I continued down the benches between the oarsmen, intent on getting to the bow without tripping.

I nearly made it. But at the third to last bench, where a heavyset, sweating man with a badly slashed nose sat beside an older, wiry man in a loincloth, I took off just as the ship pitched and landed on my bad foot. Caught off balance, my feet got tangled in both oars on the return stroke, and I slipped, smashing my shin painfully on the edge of the bench. The sweating man snarled at me.

"Curse you, you little *skatophage*—" he broke off as his bench companion shouted, "Break stroke! Break stroke!"

As if the oars were yoked together, all fifty oarsmen suddenly halted their stroke and lifted their oars from the water, the handles resting across their laps, the oars pointing straight out to the side. I scrambled across the remaining two benches and reached the foredeck.

When I got there, Ury scowled at me and spat over the side. Lopex spoke. "Twenty-three benches, Ury. Close enough. That's a skin of wine you owe me. We'll shift it in the hold after we make landfall on Ismaros."

He turned to me. "Next time get the whole way without falling, boy. I'm not breaking stroke again for a clumsy ship's boy."

My shins were smarting painfully, and an angry flush rose on my face. "This was just a bet?"

A powerful backhand blow smashed me to the deck. Ury

was standing over me, glowering. "You watch your mouth, you little piece of *kopros.*"

I tried to scramble out of the way as he aimed a couple of vicious kicks at me, stopping only when Lopex came up behind him.

"Don't break him, Ury," he said. "We need him to work." He knelt beside me. "Much more than a bet, boy," he said coldly. "If you want to live, you'll pin back that tongue. Now jump back to the stern and tell the steersmen to be prepared for landing signals—we make landfall within two hands. Move."

Back at the stern, the talkative steersman cackled. "Mouthed off to old Ury, did you? Not smart, boy. But at least you can still talk. And you didn't do too bad on the benches. Our last ship's boy, he didn't do so good. Slipped at number four."

Chapter 7

EARLY THAT EVENING, the navigator guided us to a stony beach for the night. The orb of Helios was setting through pink clouds above the western horizon. A small river flowed through the hills from a cypress valley that opened onto the beach, leading back to a blue-tinged mountain in the distance.

Lopex had ordered that the ships be beached stern-first, to loud grumbles from the rowers. "Stop," he called to the men who were hauling the ship up onto the rocky shore. "Leave her prow a few paces below the high tide mark. Put the mast up and leave the sail furled but ready to raise."

Nearby, the other ships that had left Troy behind us were

following his lead, pulling up in a crisp line on the beach, their soldiers pouring down the centre ladders and splashing into the shallows. Lopex stood on the steering deck, the ship canted over as it leaned into the ash rods that propped it up. As the last of the soldiers climbed down the ladder, he walked to the stern rail and raised his voice.

"Men of Ithaca! At last the great war is over. Within a month, with the gods' favour, we will be back home with our loved ones." He paused to let the men cheer.

"It has been a long and brutal war. Each of us has called the death names of brothers, cousins and close friends. But at last it is over! Troy is destroyed, the thousand ships bound for home. Fair Helen has been returned to her rightful husband, and the honour of the house of Atreus restored. But most important—every man here is returning home rich!" He paused as the men cheered again.

"But the war has given you more than wealth: each of you has been sculpted into a battle-hardened warrior. We now have before us a perfect chance to put those skills to use. A short march from here is the town of Maronia, at the foot of the mountain of Ismaros. Allies of that blackened heap of rubble once known as Troy. A fatal mistake! Tomorrow morning, at first light, we will march on the town and sack it." The cheers that greeted this were quieter and died out quickly.

"Unlike what we were told at Troy, this will truly be a quick assault. The town is unfortified. Its inhabitants, the Cicones, are unprepared. But"—he leaned over the rail to peer down at them—"we *must* be in and out by noon and set sail before the Cicones can regroup. Short swords and hatchets only: this is close-quarters work. Archers, leave your bows and quivers on the stern deck of your ship. No cooking fires tonight, the wind is onshore." He pointed. "Post sentries two hundred paces up the valley and the stream bed. Trench anyone who approaches. We march at first light."

There was no cheering this time, but Lopex didn't seem to notice. He turned and went down the ladder amidships.

I spent all evening lugging heavy goatskin bags of water from the river to refill the ship's cistern. One of the soldiers explained that with river water, you had to add some wine before drinking it. "It's a sacrifice to the river spirit, boy. Don't skip that unless you want him angry. Angry enough to taint the water and make us all sick, sometimes."

With the cistern full, I was immediately ordered onto the ship to help grind wheat. "See that basket?" the guard grunted as I climbed down into the hold. "Tell your Trojan friends nobody gets out until it's full."

Two other slaves looked resentful as I translated, but Zosimea, the sharp-faced woman who had advised me not to run, was unmoved. "You're both alive, aren't you?" she said tartly, her arm methodically working the *pestillos*. "And that's more than can be said for many." She dropped another handful of grain into her mortar bowl. "Now keep grinding. I'm not filling this basket by myself."

Beside her, the older man who had spoken to me on the

beach nodded. "We've been fortunate. At least with Odysseus as our master, the archers won't use us as human targets."

Odysseus? I looked up. "I thought they called him Lopex."

The older man shook his head. "That's just a nickname. His men have called him that for as long as I can remember. That is to say," he added, "since the Greeks first attacked us ten years ago."

I stared at him. Back in Troy, even I'd heard the name of Odysseus the trickster. It was said he told two lies with every breath. Then again, what I'd heard about the other Greek commanders was worse.

At someone's request, I translated what Lopex had said when we landed.

"Can't you men keep working while you talk?" Zosimea snapped at us. "No, not like that," she added, exasperated. "You're not killing roaches, for Hera's sake. Twist, don't pound."

It was well into the night before we had filled the basket and crept out of the hold, my savagely aching wrists adding to the pain in my toes and shin. Despite the chill and the dew that had soaked the ground, slaves didn't get blankets, of course, so we ended up packing ourselves in a row on the beach like wooden spoons in a basket. I found myself wedged between a loose-skinned older man in a loincloth with a loud voice and a louder snore, and Zosimea, who jerked awake violently every few minutes, groaning and jabbing me in the stomach with her elbow.

After the night's chill, an early morning mist spread from

the river valley. Someone kicked us awake and ordered us to fetch the soldiers a cold breakfast of figs and dried fish from storage. I was about to scrounge something for myself when Lopex called.

"Boy! Now!"

I trudged wearily over to where he was holding a pair of grieves. "Tie these on," he said, extending a leg. The heavy bronze plates were shiny with oil, and I struggled not to drop them. Nearby, the other soldiers were getting into their own armour. For all that Lopex had said about being a trained fighting force, no two of them wore the same thing. Most were missing grieves, arm guards or bronze collars, and much of what they still had was dented and worn, helmets missing plumes, leather straps broken and re-knotted. Ten years of war hadn't been kind to the Greeks either.

After they marched up the valley, leaving only a few soldiers to guard us, I set about pilfering some breakfast from the ship's stores and sat down on a fallen log someone had dragged into camp. I had begun to brood about my sister again when Zosimea and the greying man who'd spoken to me on the beach sat down nearby, talking. Most of the captives looked familiar—I'd seen them around Troy—but I didn't recognize his face. Well, it was a big place.

Zosimea grunted as she tore some flesh from a smoked fish with her teeth. "That Greek tramp? Can't see what you men saw in her, myself. Her and her *Greek* ways." She spat out the word like a bone.

"Mind, I don't know what old Lopex meant about her

rightful husband," she added. "From what I heard, she didn't take her hands off that fancy-boy of hers since Chryses made sacrifice at their wedding. Wouldn't let him alone, the hussy."

The man shook his head seriously. "That's the story Prince Paris put about—that Helen came back with him from the Greek islands as a virgin bride—but there's more to it."

I sat up to listen. I'd seen Helen once or twice myself, up on the wall with her husband Paris, one of King Priam's many sons. Just thinking about her sent my pulse racing. She had to be fifteen years older than I was, but I'd never seen a woman even half as good looking. Perfect high cheekbones, almond eyes, smooth—

His voice brought me back. "The truth is, Paris isn't her first husband, he's her second."

Zosimea snorted as she gnawed at her smoked fish. "Hah! What killed the first one? Overuse?"

The man ignored her. "Her first husband isn't dead. Technically, they're still married."

"Aha! I knew it, the little tramp!" Zosimea crowed.

I jumped in. "Was that what Lopex was talking about?"

He nodded, turning to me. "That's why w—" he coughed and started again "—why the Greeks went to war against us. King Agamemnon wanted to bring Helen back to her first husband, his brother Menelaus."

Zosimea choked on her fish. "*That's* what all this was

about? Ten years of war, because his brother couldn't satisfy that little minx?"

The man shrugged. "Well, that was the excuse. But the real reason was different. Why do you think Troy was so rich?"

I made a rude noise. As long as I could remember, Troy had been a war-starved dump.

He glanced over at me. "Before the war, I mean. You wouldn't remember, but Troy was rich. From where it sat, it controlled the only water route to the Sea of Propontis. Troy took a share of the cargo from every Greek trading ship that went past."

He sat back to chew on a sprig of wild oregano to clean his breath. "That's what the Greeks were really after. Control of trade routes."

Shaking her head, Zosimea tossed the fish skeleton into the fire, picked clean. "Kassander, I can't think where you find these stories. Next you'll be saying that the whole thing was the fault of the gods."

Shortly after noon I heard voices. The raiding party was tramping noisily back through the cypress valley just off the beach, their armour clanking. As they approached, I caught snatches of their conversation.

"What were they thinking? Where were the men?"

"Out in the back fields with the sheep, of course!" There was a roar of laughter.

The raiding party emerged from the valley. As they neared the camp, another voice called out. "Hey, Elpie boy! Guess what we got you! Baby clothes!" This time the laughter was even louder.

Every man was carrying something: goatskin bags of wine, brass plates, armour or other plunder. Some of the soldiers had stolen donkeys and carts that they'd loaded with heavier items. As the stream of men continued to spill from the river valley onto the beach, more men appeared, driving shambling cattle before them. They would never fit on the ships. I wondered what they were planning.

I soon found out. Within a few minutes, cooking fires had been lit from the shipboard fire pots, and the soldiers, their armour already stripped off, had begun to slaughter and skin the animals. Others were distributing goatskin bags of wine and some small, round loaves from a wagon. The noise grew rapidly.

A little while later, Lopex arrived with the final wave of returning soldiers, dragging a reluctant grey donkey by its halter as it pulled a rattling cart loaded with wine skins. He stared around the beach for a moment.

"Men!" he called. "What are you doing? Load the ships and clear the beach immediately!"

The din of celebration was too loud for him to be heard, so he climbed onto our ship and called out from the stern, his voice booming across the camp. "Fellow Achaeans! Listen to me! Our victory today was swift and simple for one reason: we followed a plan. But the plan is not yet complete. We must be off the beach before the Cicones can counterattack. Load the ships and prepare to sail!"

A few men glanced up, but most couldn't hear, or didn't care. He tried again, louder. "Men of Ithaca! Ask yourselves: why was this so easy? Because we caught them unprepared! But that will not last. Since we attacked this morning, they will have sent runners to nearby villages. Those villages are now sending reinforcements. Our strength is speed, not size. We must be gone before they return in force."

He was a strong speaker, but the wine was stronger. The soldiers near me were dismissive. "We kicked them senseless! The way we beat them, they won't come out of their villages until spring!"

I shook my head. Greek army discipline. Not that ours had been much better. Suddenly Lopex caught sight of me on the beach. "Boy! Come here!"

He pointed down at the cart he had brought back. "Unload this cart and stow it in the stern hold of the *Pelagios*." He stalked off down the beach.

I glanced over as Kassander emerged from the shade of the ship. He caught my puzzled expression. "What's the matter?"

I gestured at Lopex a little distance away, now picking up some breastplates from the sand and heading toward a knot of men squirting wine over each another from goatskins. "I'm supposed to put this stuff in a—what was it? A *Pelagios*. What's he talking about?"

Kassander patted the overlapping wooden planks of the hull beside us. "This, of course. Lopex's ship."

"He named his ship?" I peered closely at him. "Come on, don't grease the goat. What is it, really?"

He shook his head. "I'm serious. Ships always have names." He added quickly, "I mean—Greek ships do." He clapped his palms together. "So. What was Lopex saying to the men?"

I told him and he nodded thoughtfully.

"All these little coastal villages come to one another's defence," he said. "I expect he's right—the Cicones are probably heading this way right now."

I climbed the ladder gingerly and dropped the first wine skin on deck. It landed with a thud that was hardly audible above the noise from the beach. A thought struck me and I called down to him. "Will they make us fight?"

He shook his head up at me. "No. They won't put weapons in a slave's hands. Not until they're sure they've beaten our spirit out. But," he added, "Lopex may use you to carry messages in battle."

I shuddered as I came back down. "What should I do?"

"If I were you, I'd help him. If he's right—and his nickname isn't 'the fox' for nothing—then the best thing we can do is help the Greeks win. If the Cicones win, they might well kill both of us too."

"Kill us? Why? We're—" I choked on the word "—slaves."

Kassander shrugged. "We could be soldiers in disguise.

They'll play it safe. That's what the Greeks would do."

I thought about it as I finished loading Lopex's stolen goods, but it wasn't until later that it occurred to me to wonder how a Trojan knew so much about Greek strategy.

Once the last skin was up the ladder, I balanced it on the stern railing and draped one arm across it. If Lopex came by it would look like I was just taking a breather. The few clouds providing occasional shade had drifted away, and the afternoon sun was making me squint. As I leaned against the rail, I spotted a flash among the green trees of the river valley, then more. I peered harder. That wasn't sunlight on the river, it was bronze. Bronze armour.

I looked around urgently for Lopex but he was away off up the beach, forcing armour onto a group of sceptical swordsmen in loincloths. I called anyway, waving my arms, but he couldn't hear me. The Cicones were clearly visible now through the trees. They'd be emerging onto the beach any second. Were the Greeks all blind?

I waved my arms angrily from the deck. "Hey, Greeks! Look over there!" I pointed. A few of the nearer men looked up. But I was just a slave, and they returned to their wine. For a moment I was tempted to give up. Serve them right if they were slaughtered. But recalling Kassander's warning, I tried again.

As I waved at them, my toe kicked the bronze fire pot at the stern, making me wince. The Greeks kept two shielded oil lamps burning at all times to light their cooking fires from. I frowned for a moment as I stared at it, an idea coming to me. Dashing over to the benches, I began rummaging through a stash of looted plates beneath them until I spotted a small bronze goblet. Perfect. I yanked it out and tied it to one end of a cast-off rowing loincloth, then poured some of the yellow lamp oil onto it and thrust the tip into the flame.

"Hey! Greeks!" Standing at the rail, I spun the goblet in the burning cloth over my head like a sling before releasing them both to fly toward the Ciconian army, now emerging from the trees. Long practice at bringing down birds for supper had given me a strong throwing arm, and weighted by the goblet, the bundle soared over the Greeks, the burning cloth fluttering like a tail.

Even drunk, the soldiers who saw it fly overhead turned automatically to mark its fall, while others turned to follow their gaze. There was a momentary silence as they absorbed what they were looking at. Then the entire camp erupted in a flurry of yells and activity as the Greeks bolted for their weapons.

Bronze blazing in the sun, the Cicones swept down on the encampment like avenging Furies. A soldier at the edge of the camp stared drunkenly at the approaching army just a little too long. A moment later his head came spinning through the air, sliced from his shoulders by a Ciconian battle axe, blood spraying from it in a grisly arc. I saw two other Greek soldiers die in the first few seconds, one spitted through the eye with a Ciconian spear, the other slashed open from unarmoured shoulder to waist. He stared wide-eyed as his intestines spilled out onto the ground, then collapsed on top of them.

I decided I'd stay where I was.

But Lopex was right about one thing: the Greeks had experience. Their drunken stupor shaken off, they immediately formed a defensive line, fronted by the men who had gotten their armour on first, and slowed the Ciconian advance to a crawl. I stood up at the stern rail for a better look. The air was on fire with the ringing clash of sword on shield, shouts and agonized screams. Every few moments brought another cry of *khalash*! It was a shock to realize that the cry came from Ciconian warriors whenever they drew blood.

There must have been three Cicones to every Greek, but the Greek shoulder-to-shoulder formation was preventing the Cicones from bringing their numbers to bear. All the same, powered by sheer rage, the attackers were gradually pushing the Greeks off the beach toward the ships. I wondered what else the Greeks had done to make them so furious.

Lopex was dragging a wounded soldier out of the battle when he spotted me on the stern deck and waved an arm. Angry with myself for not staying hidden, I climbed down the ladder. Blood was pouring from a cut under his eye and he was sweating like the Helios horse, but his voice was calm. He leaned down and spoke into my ear, pointing. "Do you see the captain of the archers over there, the tall man with the tusk helmet and the red horsehair plume?"

I nodded. Giving me messages for him and several others, he clapped me hard on the shoulder, spinning me around and powerfully shoving me on my way before I could object. "Now get moving!"

As I staggered off, he called to me again. "Oh, and boy? Nice trick with the burning rag."

I stared at the struggling mass of men. Walk into that? I'd sooner walk into Hades. Which was where I'd find myself if I did as he asked. Could I just ignore him? The Cicones clearly had the upper hand, their fearsome *khalash!* ringing out continuously across the battlefield.

I watched anxiously, hoping the battle would break one way or the other, but Lopex spotted me. Frowning, he jerked his head angrily toward the front line, waving his knife.

There was no doubt what would happen if I disobeyed any longer. I crept up nervously behind the surging mass of warriors, noting the captain of the archers, took a deep breath and plunged in, head down. Within moments a bronze shield had smashed me in the temple. An elbow preparing a sword thrust jabbed me in the stomach, and I doubled over to be knocked to the ground and stepped on heavily by a Greek soldier dodging a Ciconian spear. Someone screamed hoarsely behind me and a heavy hand thumped onto my back—and then slid wetly to the ground.

Gagging, I struggled to my hands and knees and was halfway to my feet when a sword slashed wickedly just above my head, clanging off someone's armour. I dropped back to the ground, sweating. It suddenly came to me that I was safer down here: most of the action was up at sword height.

I began to worm through the tangle of sweating, greave-bound legs, belly to the ground. Any soldiers who saw me were too preoccupied with the battle to worry about a weaponless boy. Even so, I took several bad kicks in the side and a painful stamp on the hand before rising to my feet next to the plumed captain of the archers.

"Great Zeus, boy, where did you come from?" he exclaimed, pausing to parry a vicious thrust from a Ciconian soldier in a collarless breastplate, slicing his neck open with the return slash. Hot blood spurted from the Cicone's neck as he collapsed, spattering my face.

I sputtered but bawled my message quickly in his ear, then dropped and slithered out of the front lines. The second man I spoke to nodded crisply and spun to comply, but when I reached Ury, he stared wildly at me for a moment before he seemed to understand. I slipped away before he could think to send a reply.

Safely behind the lines, I scrambled back up to the stern deck of the *Pelagios* before Lopex could assign something more. The other slaves were huddled in the hold, but I stayed above to watch the plan unfold.

The first phase was a disaster. As fifty men were pulled

from the front lines and climbed aboard their ships, the Cicones seized the chance to push the remaining Greek fighters back down the beach, ever closer to the water. The shouts and screams grew even louder as they approached.

But the Greek bows were lined up at the stern rails as though it had been planned that way, and as each soldier came on board, he grabbed his bow and immediately started shooting. Now I understood why they'd been pulled out: they were the archers.

Arrows from all ships began hissing into the Ciconian ranks like wasps, forcing them to hold their tall bronze shields over their heads and exposing them to the slashing Greek swords. Shooting from above with the Cicones this close, the Greek archers couldn't miss. Maybe it wasn't as much of a disaster as I'd thought. Quick to seize the advantage, the defending Greeks halted their retreat and began to beat the Cicones back from the ships again.

Now the Cicones tried a new tactic. A volley of flashing arrows arced up toward us from the rear of the Ciconian ranks, passing over the archers' heads to land on the deck behind me. Missed. As the Greek archers returned fire on the unshielded Ciconian bowmen, I smirked, but then I looked back and realized they hadn't been aiming at people.

Most of the arrows had overshot the ship, but several had landed on the deck behind me. Their heads were wrapped in rags and coated in burning pitch, and as they landed on the stern deck, the fire leapt to the wood. My mouth went dry as the flames began to spread. I glanced back at the archers, but they were preoccupied at the stern rail. The onboard water cistern was below decks at the other end of the ship: too far.

The fires were still small, but the dry deck was catching fast. Whipping off my father's tattered *chiton* I squatted and began to beat at the nearest flames. The ugly scent of scorched wool filled my nostrils, but the flames were out. I leapt to the second, then the third. It had fallen between the benches and landed on a sack of millet. With what remained of my *chiton*, I beat its flames out as well.

Panting, I held up the tattered garment. Scorched or burnt through in a dozen places, it was nearly useless. I was about to throw it over the side, but the thought of being naked in front of men like Ury stopped me. I threw it back over my shoulders and wrapped it as best I could.

As I did, the deck lurched violently. Had the Cicones reached the ship? I rushed to the stern rail and peered over, worming my way between the sweating archers.

A glance told me the battle wasn't going well, at least not for the Greeks. More men had been pulled from the battle, this time to push the ships back off the beach, and the small number of Greeks still in the front line were being rapidly forced back. The Cicones were now so close that I could make out the designs embossed on their breastplates. At least our archers had stopped the fire arrows.

But it was the Greeks who were rocking the *Pelagios* as

they heaved it off the beach. High tide had been just past noon and the sea had drawn off since, leaving the ships stranded high on the shallow beach. I clung to the railing as the men strained at the ropes, making the ship shudder as it scraped awkwardly down the pebbles and into the water.

With a sudden surge, the *Pelagios* floated free, and Phidios, the thick-lipped rowing master, scrambled up the ladder, panting. "You! Help me deploy the boarding nets!"

I stared at him. What was he talking about? "Oh, for Athene's sake," he grunted. "Like this."

Straddling two benches, he reached under the railing to grab a rolled net of twisted ox-hide and threw it over the side. I looked again in surprise and realized that it was unrolling as it fell, one end firmly tied below the rail. He gestured at the railing near me.

"Now do the same thing on the port side. Get going!"

I moved reluctantly to obey as the remaining Greek soldiers began splashing into the waist-deep water to swarm up the nets. The Cicones, realizing their advantage, had pushed the defending Greeks right to the water's edge, but with no defenders in the way, the archers at the stern now had a clear field of fire, their bowstrings snapping off shots as quickly as the men could string them. The sudden withering hail of arrows forced the Cicones to a halt, giving the last Greek soldiers time to splash out to the ship. I couldn't help a small smile at the sight of the plunder from Maroneia scattered across the beach. The Greeks were leaving it all behind.

Lopex was the last to board. The Cicones, after a moment of hesitation, started out into the water after us, holding their shields up to protect their heads. Lopex glanced up toward the mast.

"Get that sail up!" he shouted. The men needed no urging. Having committed themselves, the Cicones were coming out fast. With the mast already in place, the sail was hauled up by its ropes in moments and began filling with wind.

Looking back at the beach in the late afternoon sun, I could see at least two dozen Greek soldiers lying there, dead or dying. Many of them were missing an arm or leg. In the pitched battle, nobody had been available to bind or cauterise their wounds. Three Ciconian warriors were walking along the beach, two kneeling to hold down each dying Greek soldier by his shoulders, while the third stabbed him carefully through each eye with his spear.

"Pull in those boarding nets!" Lopex shouted as he pulled up the centre ladder. This time I scrambled to obey. I didn't want the Cicones boarding us either. As I reached the stern, I noticed a lone Greek soldier in the water behind us, struggling to catch up with the ship, now cutting a visible swath through the grey water. His helmet and shield were missing, but his oversized breastplate and sword were weighing him down as he struggled to swim. He'd be out of reach of the stern boarding net in a few seconds. I leaned on the rail, watching. Behind him, the Cicones had given up the chase as the ships reached deeper water, and were wading back to the beach.

He was going to drown. His armour was too heavy, he was too tired. I wondered why he didn't drop the large sword across his back. His head rolled as he started to go under, and he looked directly up at me for an instant, his eyes exhausted.

He was a boy, no older than me. I hesitated. Was there nobody else? But there were no Greeks near me, the archers having gone forward to help the wounded unlace their armour. I wanted to stay where I was, but from somewhere inside me, a deeper voice was demanding that I act.

Irritated, I jumped over the rail and scrambled down the stern boarding net, still trailing in the water behind the ship. As I reached the end, I hooked my arms into it and kicked my legs back to float free. I had never learned to swim, and the feeling was unsettling.

"Hey! Greek! Grab my feet!" I shouted. His head was already underwater so I kicked out at him. My foot clipped his chin and I felt a hand grab my ankle, a weak grip already starting to slip. I unhooked one arm from the boarding net, reached down and grabbed for his wrist. Pulling hard, I dragged him up and hooked his arms into the net beside me. We trailed in the foaming seawater behind the ship for a moment as I tried to catch my breath.

From above, I heard Lopex's voice. "Boy! Why is this net still down?" His head appeared over the stern railing, but his angry expression changed as he caught sight of us. He leapt over the rail and scrambled down the net. Carrying the half-drowned soldier under one arm, he climbed back up one-handed and disappeared over the railing. He didn't come back for me, of course. My resentment seethed as I struggled back up on my own. When I reached the deck, I was taken aback for a moment. Lopex was kneeling over the soldier, carefully taking off his armour to help him breathe. He looked up and his eyes flickered over my half-burnt *chiton*.

"Elpenor," he said, "this is the slave who saved you."

The boy opened his mouth to speak, but his body was wracked by a sudden spasm of coughing. When it was over, he looked up and gripped my hand weakly. "Pen," he wheezed. "Call me Pen."

Chapter 8

"LOOK AT THE SUN!" The navigator waved a hand skyward, where Helios was now creeping down to the western horizon. "And the charts hold no harbours after Abdera until beyond Thasos, another half-day's sailing!" He stabbed at the sheepskin chart with an agitated finger.

Lopex's back was to me, his arms folded, but from my seat on the bow deck, I had no trouble catching the navigator's reply. "At night? Are you mad? How can I navigate when I can't see the land? And there'll be no moon until second watch tonight. We could sail right onto a reef and not know it until the crabs are up our backsides!" He struggled for calm. "Look, I know we have to beach away from

Ismaros. But I'll tell you straight, Lopex, I'd rather take on the whole Ciconian army than be caught on unfamiliar water after dark."

Lopex paused, then gave a curt nod. So just after sunset, Procoros directed us to a secluded cove. High, reddish cliffs rose sheer from behind a narrow, sandy beach, no more than a half-day's sail from the beach at Ismaros. While the Greeks ate, we spent the evening hauling heavy skins of water from a spring at the base of the cliff to refill the ship's cistern. It was well past midnight before I was done, too tired even to scrounge scraps for supper. I wormed my way into the tangle of snoring slaves and was asleep in moments.

It felt like I had hardly gotten to sleep when I was kicked awake again to a grey, foggy dawn. I staggered to my feet, still wearing the mangled *chiton* that was my only garment, but Zosimea didn't comment as we were set to work making the usual morning meal of boiled millet porridge. The big bronze pots held a lot—back in Troy I'd seen vessels that size used to boil whole sheep—and I was sent for more water with a handful of goatskins.

Ury was sitting on a rock picking bits of last night's cold stew from under his fingernails with a knife. He stepped into my way as I approached. "Watch where you're walking, boy!" he growled. My burnt *chiton* caught his attention. "What did you do, slave? Jump into a fire?" He grabbed my shoulder as I went around him. "Try this one!" He gave me a powerful shove that sent me staggering toward a nearby cooking fire. My foot snagged on a tuft of beach grass and I pitched headlong into the flames.

Snatching up my hands to break my fall, I landed on the goatskins. They sizzled as my weight pushed them down into the coals, and I felt a sharp pain in my knuckles. I rolled frantically out of the fire, wincing. The smell of burning hair wasn't entirely from the empty skins, and I reached up to beat at my smouldering scalp. Zosimea dashed over with some water in a small green *kylix*, pouring some on my head and face, then grabbed my hand and plunged my knuckles into what was left. Rolling out quickly had spared me a worse burn, but along with my knuckles, my face and one shoulder stung as though from a bad sunburn. I spun around angrily, knocking the water from Zosimea's hands.

Ury laughed unpleasantly. "That was clumsy, boy! You've put the fire out!"

Heedless of Zosimea's restraining tug, I snarled back at him, "You brainless Greek barbarian! You should have died in Troy with your brother!"

Ury's laughter stopped. "What did you say, boy?"

A warning flickered in my mind, but I was too angry to heed it. "You heard me! If I had a knife I'd see you to Hades myself!"

He stared at me as though he couldn't believe what he'd heard. His expression changed as it sank in. "I warned you, boy," he growled, reaching for his knife. "I told you what I'd do if you ever spoke like that again to me."

"You little fool!" Zosimea hissed at me, looking at Ury's expression. "What did you say to him?" As Ury started toward me, she grabbed my arm. "Go for water, boy, and be sure you take a long time coming back!" She gave me a push that sent me staggering.

From behind me I caught Ury's snarl. "You get back here, slave!" At least he wasn't coming after me. Lazy barbarian.

The tan skins that had saved me from a worse burn were now blackened lumps in the fire behind me, so I circled around to grab some others from the hold. Picking my way over the rockfall at the base of the cliff, I made my way to the spring in a stand of scraggly willows at the base of the cliff. I lay down to rinse my burning face and knuckles in the water. It had a strange metallic taste, like blood. Why had I shouted at Ury? Stupid. Just stupid. Even if he had pushed me into a fire. Why couldn't I control my tongue?

My burns gradually stopped aching, and I rolled over into the grass to watch the clouds scudding across the sky, breaking up the sunlight. Eventually, a slave from another ship came for water, and I stood up to return. Threading the loops on the skins through an ash branch, I balanced the load across my shoulders and headed back to camp. The base of the cliff behind the beach was strewn with rubble, and I picked my way awkwardly across it. It took longer, but at least from this direction Ury couldn't sneak up on me. I kept an eye out for him as I entered the camp, but he wasn't around.

Many of the soldiers were awake by now, but Elpenor was still asleep on a scruffy blanket in the sand, a once-fine brown *chiton* over his shoulders. This was the first time I'd had a chance to see him clearly. He was slender and delicate-looking, with narrow shoulders and smooth-skinned hands, his large eyes set into a small, pale face. A very handsome boy, nearly pretty. Just the type to become the butt of abuse in a camp of hardened soldiers. I realized with a jolt who the Elpie was that I'd heard the soldiers mocking yesterday.

Even in sleep, his face had a pinched, unhappy look, and I couldn't help feeling sorry for him. His left thigh, poking out from his tunic, was wrapped in a filthy bandage, badly tied and soaked with blood. The bandage was half off, dark streaks just starting up his leg under the skin. I recalled my father once pointing them out on a soldier he was treating. "You see those, Alexias?" he had said quietly. "The Egyptians call them the fingers of *eksepsis*. They reach in through the wound. If I don't stop them, they'll reach straight for his heart and pull out his soul."

I glanced around at the other soldiers. Everywhere I looked, men were wearing dirty bandages, most tied badly and stained dark with blood, mementos of yesterday's botched battle. Other wounds weren't bandaged at all. I shook my head. Greek medicine.

Just then I caught Ury's gravelly voice nearby, so I took off to dump my water into the pot. As I waited for it to boil, I heard Lopex speaking quietly to someone. "How bad is he?"

The other man spoke. "He's unconscious. A lot of blood came out during the night. I don't know if he'll ever wake."

Lopex grunted. "Keep it to yourself. It won't help the men to know their healer is dying."

Well, that explained why their wounds had been bound so badly. And without a healer to treat him, Elpenor—Pen—would probably die too. I stared into the blackened bronze pot, watching a few bubbles spiral to the surface as the water heated. If the whole Greek army died I wouldn't lose any sleep. But from the way I'd seen the men treat him, Pen seemed just as trapped here as I was.

Trapped. At the thought, an image of my sister lying crumpled at the bottom of the stairs invaded my thoughts. Suddenly my face was wet with sweat, my heart pounding. A surge of terror gripped me like a fist. The Greeks were coming up the stairs after me. I had to get out! I glanced around. Greek soldiers on all sides. There was a cluster of small cypress trees just off the beach; if I could reach that I could hide. I tried to run but my legs wouldn't move. Any moment now the soldiers would spot me. Why hadn't they already?

My legs unlocked and I stumbled, landing on my knees in the sand. I stayed where I was for a few moments as normal thought slowly crept back.

What had just happened? For a moment I had been right back in Troy, on *that* night. I didn't dare think about it, terrified that it might happen again. For a little while I lay

curled on the ground, waiting for the shaking to pass, trying to think of something else as the sweat cooled on my forehead.

Sounds from the pot roused me. I stood up, my knees shaky. The water had come to a powerful boil, and I wondered how long I'd been . . . elsewhere. I glanced around, but none of the soldiers nearby seemed to have noticed. Whatever it had been, I was glad it was over.

I'd saved Pen once. I'd be cursed if I was going to let him die now. Even if he was a Greek. I gave the pot an angry stir. The sight reminded me of my father boiling water in his *xeneon*. A memory surfaced. Perhaps there was something I could do.

Scrounging a torn tunic from the hold, I ripped it into several strips and dropped them into the boiling water. My father had never said how long it took, so I waited a while before fishing them out with a stick and wrapping them in a separate cloth. I dumped the end of a sailcloth sack of millet into the pot and went off to find Pen.

Kneeling beside him, I unwound his filthy, sodden bandage. Fully visible, the wound was even worse, a long, ragged gash through his thigh muscle, the skin on either side a fiery red. It was encrusted with sand and dried blood, and the smell had attracted sandflies. Holding the boiled white cloth with a dry one, I wiped the dirt and insects away. It was starting to come back to me.

Pen woke up. "Ow!" he said, jerking his leg away and

getting more sand in it. "What are you doing, slave?"

"Stop moving, would you?" I said, irritated. "This wound will kill you if it isn't treated. Your healer can't do it, he's halfway to Hades."

"Kallikrates? But he isn't even sick!"

I shook my head. "Not sick. Wounded. In the battle yesterday."

Pen stared at me. "But he shouldn't have been fighting at all. He's just a healer."

"That's right," I grunted. "Now be quiet a moment." I concentrated.

"Clean wound, clean bandages, air and time," my father's voice came back to me. I continued wiping the dirt and dried blood away with the tunic I had just boiled.

"Hey!" Pen yelped. "That's hot!"

"Keep your voice down," I muttered. "Do you want everyone to hear?"

"But it *hurts*!" he replied, his eyes filling with tears. "Aren't healers supposed to make it feel *better*?"

"It's something my father always did," I said. "He was a healer. He said the heat helped. I don't know why." I finished wiping the dirt out of the wound as Pen whimpered, then wrapped it with a second strip and tied it off as my father had shown me.

As I stood up to go, he called, "Slave?"

I turned.

"Thank you," he said awkwardly. "For saving my life.

Back at Ismaros. And this." He gestured to his bandage.

I shrugged. "Keep it clean." I walked away to keep him from saying anything more.

I looked around for Ury as I stirred the lumpy porridge, wondering why I'd just done that. Pen was one of *them*. He'd most likely killed someone I knew. Why did I care what happened to him? Watching the thick bubbles burst on the surface of the porridge, I let my attention wander.

A massive hand grabbed my shoulder and roughly yanked me around. It was Ury, his grimy, black-haired face inches from mine. "I told you what I'd do to you, boy," he snarled, his meaty fingers squeezing my shoulder hard. "I'll cut that sharp tongue of yours right out of your mouth."

Dropping me behind the cooking tripod with the same quick move he'd used to capture me, he fell heavily on me, pulling my jaw open with one filthy paw while he pulled out his knife with the other.

I struggled to yell, to scream, to bite, but with his huge hand grappling for my tongue I could barely squeak. He slid the long bronze hunting blade between my teeth, slicing savagely into the corner of my mouth. Gods—he was really going to do it! Desperate, I struggled to push his arm away, but he was unstoppable.

"Open up boy, or I'll cut right through your cheek," he grunted, his breath hot on my face. The sharp edge of his dagger was sawing deeper into the side of my tongue. Heedless of the fresh burst of agony it caused, I clamped my teeth hard on his blade, taking some pressure off my tongue but levering the edge deeper into my cheek and releasing a further gush of blood down my throat.

My flailing left hand struck something and I snatched it up, a thick olive-wood branch from the cooking fire, the other end glowing. Without pausing to think I stabbed it at his face. It sizzled where it struck. Ury roared and clapped a hand to his cheek, letting go of his knife, and I snatched up a handful of sand to throw into his eyes. He rolled off me, rubbing his eyes and cheek at the same time.

I scrambled to my feet and ran. Gods, what had I done? Any slave knew that attacking a free man meant instant death. Running blindly through the camp, I tripped over Elpenor, still stretched out on his blanket, and fell on my face in the sand. Bronze-hard fingers gripped my shoulder and hauled me upright. "What's going on here, boy?" a voice barked. It was Lopex.

I began to stammer a reply, but Ury charged up. "Do you know what that filthy little scut did? He attacked me! He's a vicious little cur. I warned you he was feral, Lopex. Didn't I warn you?"

I squirmed frantically to get free but Lopex didn't notice. "He attacked you?"

"Look at this!" Ury pulled his hand away to show a patch of burnt beard surrounding an angry red blister. "He'll never train, Lopex. Give him here."

Lopex held me out at arm's length for a moment. "You're right, Ury." He sounded tired. "He didn't work out. Trench him. But make it quick."

Ury grabbed me roughly by the neck and bent down to put his meaty lips beside my ear. "Quick? I don't think so," he whispered, sliding the point of his knife up my cheek. "And this time it'll be more than your tongue, boy." His knife point stopped beside my eye. "Maybe those little grey eyes next. Or—"

On the ground before us, Elpenor sat up. "Wait!" he blurted. "He's not like that! He saved my life!" He cast around desperately and his eye fell on the bandage. "Look at this! He bandaged me, where the Cicones got me yesterday!"

Lopex frowned. "Ury, hold it." He knelt to run his fingers over the wrapping on Pen's leg, then stood up and turned to me. "Boy. Did you do this?"

Ury's hand on my throat suddenly clenched so hard it cut off my breath. "The slave?" he broke in, as I struggled to speak. "Of course he didn't. Elpie's lying. Here, I'll just trench the little scut now." His knife flashed up in an arc from his waist but Lopex's hand snapped out and intercepted it a finger's width from my throat.

"I said hold, Ury," Lopex said firmly, his hand gripping Ury's wrist. "Now release him. Answer me, slave. Did you do this?"

Ury reluctantly let go of my throat, and I gasped for air. Unable to speak, I nodded, my eyes watering.

Lopex looked down at the bandage again. "This is a surgeon's knot. How did you learn this? Who taught you?"

Pen broke in. "His father! He's a healer!"

Lopex's gaze swivelled back to me. "Your father? A Trojan healer? What's his name?"

I finally caught my breath. "Aristides. Of Herakleon."

He frowned. "Tall man? Combed beard? Scar on his forehead?"

"Yes, sir, that's him. It—*was* him."

Lopex's eyebrows rose. "Him!" He paused in thought. "I knew of your father, boy. Relieved the pain for men of mine after more than one battle, Trojan and enemy though he was." His voice seemed to be coming from somewhere far off. "A waste," he added. "That arrow was a stray. We don't target healers." He turned toward me again. "So you're his son. Can you heal, boy?"

I stammered. "A bit, I guess. I helped my father with cuts and burns, and—"

He grabbed me by my burned shoulder and I winced. "Well, boy, our healer's hurt. So until he gets better or you die, you're taking his place."

Ury broke in. "What? You're making him a *healer*? He'll kill us all in our sleep!" He reached for me. "Give him here, Lopex. I'll fix him now."

Lopex grabbed Ury's wrist and clenched until Ury gasped and dropped his knife. "Listen to me, Ury," he said. "He's mouthy and disobedient. But I don't believe he would attack you unprovoked." His eyes flickered to the fresh cut at the side of my mouth, and I chose that moment to spit out a mouthful of blood.

"As long as I am commander of this expedition," he continued to Ury, "you will obey my orders. Is that clear?" Ury grunted something.

Lopex led me to the ship, pulled high on the beach, and climbed the stern boarding net behind me. "Men of Ithaca!" he called from the stern, addressing the entire camp. "Kallikrates the healer was wounded in the battle yesterday. But I have prepared for this!" He grabbed my wrist and hauled my arm into the air. "I have here the son of Aristides of Herakleon, the famous Trojan healer, who taught him all the skills of healing."

I plucked at his shoulder. "I didn't say that! He wasn't famous, and he didn't teach me that much—"

He looked down at me impatiently. "Shut up, boy. Of course he didn't. The men need to believe you know what you're doing. So make sure they never doubt it."

He lifted his head to address the camp again. "Until Kallikrates recovers, I declare this slave *hagios*. He is not to be harmed." His gaze swept over Ury before turning back to me. "Don't get ideas, boy. If any of your patients die, I'll kill you. And if you *ever* raise a hand to a free man again, I'll give you to Ury. Now start healing." He gave me a shove toward the ladder that sent me stumbling across the sloping deck.

As I picked myself up, I recalled crazy Cassie's prediction, back in Troy. *Survive. Accept your father's gift.* I'd come within a blade's breadth of being killed today. Perhaps, just once, Cassie had gotten it right.

Chapter 9

THAT EVENING WE were sitting by the slaves' campfire, eating scraps the Greeks had left. For once, the cisterns were full and our other chores done early enough that we had time to talk, although my injured tongue made it hard. Soldiers nearby were playing some kind of game by dropping rocks on each other's bellies until someone grunted. Typical Greek stupidity.

Cross-legged in the sand, Zosimea was gnawing gristle from a pig's hock when I told them what Lopex had said. She looked up from her meal. "He did? That's good news, boy. Means you're no longer a slave!"

Sitting on a piece of driftwood he had dragged over to the fire, Kassander shook his head. "He's still a slave, and his master can still withdraw *hagios* and kill him if he chooses. But," he added, "even Ury wouldn't dare transgress against *hagios*, so at least you're safe from him." He paused. "Probably."

A knot popped in the fire, and I brushed a spark from the *chiton* the fat storesmaster had given me, white wool with a pattern of gold squares along the edge. Lopex clearly didn't want his new healer in rags.

Kassander leaned forward. "Alexi? Have you treated Kallikrates, the old healer, yet?"

He sat back, satisfied, as I shook my head, my mouth full. "Good. Then you know what you have to do."

"No. What?"

Kassander looked me in the eye. "Kill him, of course."

I choked, coughing a spray of half-chewed millet into the fire. "What?" I peered through the flames at him. "You're serious, aren't you? What do I look like, an assassin?"

"Your influence with Lopex will last only as long as Kallikrates is sick," he explained patiently. "The moment he's back on his feet, you'll be back to fetching and carrying."

"But Lopex said he'd kill me if any of my patients died!"

Kassander shook his head. "That's a standard Greek threat for any slave in a position of power." He paused for a sip of water, then added, "Just don't be obvious about it."

I stared at him. "But he's just lying there!"

Kassander shrugged. "Best time for it. Or would you rather wait until he's back on his feet?"

I started to object, but he held up a hand. "Look here, to

the side of the neck. Here, where it pulses. Nick him with his own knife. Healers do it on the battlefield when the wounds are too bad. His blood will run out, and he'll die quietly in a few minutes. Your father was an expert."

"My father?" I was caught off guard. "How do you know? Did you—were you in the army before you were captured?"

He looked down. "Yes. I was a soldier," he said quietly. But he wouldn't say any more.

The next morning Lopex ordered me to examine the wounded. Some had bad slashes and stab wounds, but I discovered that I knew more than I had thought. Thank the gods there were no limbs bad enough to cut off. My father had never let me stay when he was doing amputations, but I had heard the screams.

My tongue had stiffened up to the point where it was hard to talk. Fortunately most of the taciturn Greek soldiers weren't interested in making conversation with a slave. Several of them were already showing signs of *eksepsis*: swollen, angry tissue and red streaks under the nearby skin, and in one case, the nauseating smell of rotting meat. As I rebandaged their wounds, I wondered whether they'd killed anyone I had known. The Greeks were just as suspicious of me, a healer who was not only Trojan but a slave, and a boy at that. But Lopex had spoken for me, and that seemed to count for something. Besides, as one older warrior remarked while I cleaned out a nasty gash on his chest, "Can't say I think much of your Trojan healing, boy, but Krats was no prize either."

That afternoon I was examining a soldier named Theron, one of the dark, scowling men I'd seen around Ury. His face and arms were cratered with at least a half a dozen old wounds, and there were two fresh ones on his cheek and his thigh. The thigh wound was especially deep, and had crusted over with sand and dried blood.

I pulled a boiled rag from my bundle and was about to wash his thigh when a knife flashed in front of my face. "You just put that thing down, boy. I don't need any of your *Trojan* healing. Wrap and wax, that's what it wants."

I rolled my eyes. "Fine," I said thickly. "It's no grease off my axle." The Greek method was to wipe a wound out with whatever dirty cloth was available, wrap it tightly, then pour hot wax over the bandage to seal it. With treatment like that, I couldn't see how anyone ever survived. Well, it was his leg.

As I stood up to fetch some wax from the ship's stores, I was stopped by a sudden, vivid memory from when I was very young. My father's strong, capable fingers were treating one of his patients when his voice asked me to hold one end of a long bandage while he wrapped the other around the man's forearm. My father had been passionate about his calling. I couldn't imagine him waxing a wound, even at knifepoint.

"S'matter, boy? Forget what you're doing?" Theron sneered.

"No." I looked down at him. "I think I've just remembered." I knelt and began to unwrap the bandage again.

Ignoring his yelps of pain, I set about sponging out the
dirt and dried blood from the slash. The blood was heavily
encrusted and needed hard scrubbing, inflaming the exposed flesh below. Theron wasn't one to suffer in silence.
"Apollo's *gloutos*, boy, didn't I tell you to treat me properly?"
He groped on the sand for his knife.

I glanced up from the filthy wound. "You know something, *Greek*? I wouldn't care if you died. But I'm your healer
now. I won't let your stupid prejudice keep me from doing
it the right way." I gave the wound a savage swipe with the
rag, eliciting another angry yelp. "Just be quiet or I'll walk
away and let you do it yourself." He slumped back and
glowered at me, but held his tongue.

By late afternoon I'd seen everyone else and couldn't put it
off any longer. Kallikrates was with the other badly wounded
on the edge of the camp. I knelt nervously in the sand beside him. From his greying beard and flabby arms, he was
clearly no warrior. The confusion of the battle yesterday
must have caught him in the front lines.

I unwrapped his tunic. My father had always kept his
tunics a glowing white, boiling them daily to keep them
clean, but Kallikrates' was as filthy as those of the soldiers
around him. I shrugged.

A stab wound just below his ribs had leaked dark blood

across one side of his tunic and turned the sand beneath him a sticky black. My father had once said that when the blood was dark, it was old and tired. And it was true that the bright red blood was what spurted; dark blood mostly oozed, as if its strength were gone. My father didn't miss much.

Examining the spot on his neck, I couldn't see it moving, but could feel a slow pulse under my fingers. Whatever it did, only the living had one. If I cut into it now, Kallikrates would die. The thought was shocking, horrifying, and yet somehow... invigorating. To take a Greek life. A chance for vengeance, of a sort. I licked my lips.

A hand was stealing toward the knife on Kallikrates' rope belt. Were those my fingers? Suddenly the knife was in my hand, cold bronze against my palm.

"Boy! What do you think you're doing?"

Startled, I dropped the knife and spun around. Lopex had come up behind me.

I fumbled for something to say. "I'm sorry, master. I thought, I mean, he was nearly dead anyway..." I trailed off under his gaze.

"So you thought you'd steal his knife?" Lopex's tone was sharp.

"I'm sorry, it was wrong, I know," I babbled, relief washing over me.

"Only a ghoul loots the living. The son of Aristides should have more honour than that." He reached down to tuck the knife back into Kallikrates' belt. "Get on with your duties."

As Lopex walked away, I turned back to look at the unconscious Kallikrates, stretched out helpless before me, knife glinting from his belt. My hand crept toward it once again, but stopped. This felt wrong. I reached angrily for a rag from my sailcloth bag to wipe out his wound. Lopex was right. The son of Aristides had more honour than that.

Chapter 10

THE STORM SWEPT down on us like a beast from Tartarus. Nobody noticed just when the coastline vanished in the pounding rain and spray, our whole attention consumed by bailing. As the ship climbed to the peak of each mountainous wave, it paused for a moment at the top, then dropped headlong into the trough in a sickening plunge that squeezed my stomach into a hard ball. At the bottom, the bow of the ship vanished beneath the surging grey surface for an endless moment before emerging with a fresh flood of water to be bailed out with sponges, buckets, whatever came to hand. We couldn't stop for a moment: the water had to be scooped out before we took on more at the bottom of the next trough.

The waves around us were alive with the hiss of gale-borne rain sleeting into the sea and the angry thunderbolts of father Zeus. Trapped in a monstrous struggle between the gods of sea and sky, we clung to the prayer that we were not their target. Forged on Olympus by Hephaestus the smith-god himself, the bolts of Zeus never missed.

Terrifying though the howling wind and lightning were, the noises from the ship itself were worse. As it teetered at the top of each wave, its timbers groaned like a wounded animal, threatening to split in half under the strain. The constant pitching wrung my stomach dry, disgorging what little it held. I wasn't alone: at least a third of the Greeks spent that day retching over the side.

Only a day ago, our departure had been swift and efficient. Lopex had intended to wait until the wounded men were fit for travel, but the plan changed at noon of our third day, when the beach lookout spotted a small boat with a triangular sail, cruising slowly past the inlet. As we watched, it turned around and headed back the way it came.

Lopex stared intently at the boat until it disappeared, then turned to face the camp. "Men!" he shouted. "Break camp! We sail in two hands." It took a moment before I understood. The Greeks divided the day and night into twenty hands, the time it took the sun to cross from wrist to fingertip behind a hand held at arm's length.

I caught up with Kassander, who was carrying some

empty water skins to the spring. His stoop was almost gone today. "Why is he so afraid of that little boat?" I asked him. "It didn't even come near us!"

His eyebrows went up. "Your master's no fool," he replied. "The Cicones have no navy to speak of, just some coastal fishing boats like that one. But those fishermen will report our location as soon as they return." He frowned. "Impressive, that. I've never heard of a ship that could sail into the wind before. Thank the gods they have no navy or they could manoeuvre around us as if we were stones."

He scratched his chin, thinking. "I'd guess that the Cicones will be on the march within a few hands. If they push it, they could arrive in time to mount a dawn attack tomorrow. And as you saw yesterday, beaches make a poor defensive position."

The men had learned from Ismaros, and the ships were floated swiftly enough for us to row out on the trailing end of the high tide that afternoon. But at the steering oar, the steersman Zanthos had shaken his head. "Don't like the looks of that sky," he muttered.

It wasn't long before I found out why.

It had been bad during the day, but night was worse. Daytime, we'd had a lookout watching for land ahead, a harbour for refuge or cliffs to avoid. But we found no sanctuary, and landing on a rocky shore in this storm would have been suicidal. The night, black as squid ink, could have blown us past a dozen harbours or a hundred cliffs.

The ship plunged blindly on, its timbers creaking madly on each crest as we fought to keep it above the waves, praying to any gods who might be listening that we wouldn't run aground on a reef or be battered to splinters by a rocky coast.

By the grey dawn of the second morning, my stomach had settled down enough to let me think, but the storm was as fierce as ever. "Why doesn't he take the sail down?" I bawled into the steersman's ear over the howling wind, the spray-laden gale lashing my hair against his face.

"Because we're not ready to die yet, boy!" he bellowed back through salt-cracked lips. "That sail keeps us ahead of them waves. Without it, they'd spin us broadside and swamp us out!" Glancing up at the straining mast and drum-tight sail, I caught again the eerie threnody of the wind blowing through the taut ox-hide stays and muttered a quick prayer to Poseidon. I should have known better. Of all the gods, only Hades had a stronger thirst for souls than Poseidon, lord of the seas.

It happened just after a grey dawn on the morning of the third day. The driving rain had fallen off, but the waves were still dangerously high. Two days of constant pounding had loosened the ship's seams to the point that we were stuffing our own tunics into the cracks to try to seal them, leaving the slaves and most of the Greeks in loincloths or naked. I had been bailing the bow hold with the other slaves all night, passing my bucket up the ladder to a soldier to empty over the side, and each dip of my bucket made the bilges squeak and rustle as the waterlogged hold rats scrambled out of the way. Suddenly there was a loud crack from up top.

Scrambling up the ladder, I was just in time to see the mast topple, its jagged stump stabbing upward as the billowing sail wrapped the men beneath in a clammy linen shroud. Lopex sprang up immediately to untangle the men from the sail, cutting the stay lines and heaving the shattered mast overboard in what seemed a single motion.

The steersmen were bending their oars to keep the ship from turning broadside to the waves, but without the sail it had already begun. Laden with plunder and knee-high with water in the hold, the ship was sluggish, but I could see it beginning a slew to the right. As the turn continued, the waves began to tip the ship dangerously. I grabbed something for balance as the men began to clamour in terror.

Lopex leapt to the stern deck. "We're not dead yet, men!" he shouted, his voice booming out over the wind. "And by Athene, we won't be if you do what I say! Port side, out oars! Now!" His forceful tone was compelling, and the men scrambled to unship their oars as Lopex came forward across the benches. I watched fearfully, clinging to the bow rail.

"Port side, stroke backwards! Row! Row! Row!" he called out from the bow, timing his calls to set their pace. The men on the left dipped their oars and started to row. For a moment I couldn't understand: they were rowing in the wrong direction! Then I got it. Pushing the left side backwards was counteracting the waves slewing us to the right.

Our turn slowed but didn't stop. We were now almost broadside to the oncoming sea and the ship was tipping so far as it slipped down each wave I had to cling to the railing to keep from tumbling overboard. One more large wave would spill us into the seething ocean below. Lopex responded immediately. "Port side rowers, turn around. Face the bows. Now!"

The rowers scrambled to turn around so that they faced the front of the boat. "Port side rowers, ready, row!"

Facing the other way, the rowers could pull their oars naturally instead of pushing on them. With the full strength of their backs behind their strokes, the ship slowly began to straighten. But Lopex wasn't done yet.

"Starboard side, out oars! Standard row!" On the right side of the ship, the oars were extended and began to row *in the other direction*. I watched, rapt, at the spectacle of the two banks of oarsmen rowing in opposite directions. It was working, the ship turning smoothly to reverse the slew. As the *Pelagios* slowly righted itself and the side-to-side pitching stopped, Lopex barked more orders to halt the turn. Despite the ongoing storm, the men began laughing in relief. We weren't going to sink after all! At least not yet. Phidios the rowing master, grasping the scheme, took over.

Lopex stood on the forward deck watching the rowers,

his arms folded, his sea balance superb. From the side, with the wind whipping his beard off his lantern-square jaw, he looked a bit like my father.

I took a deep breath. "Sir?"

He turned, a scowl just starting across his face, and I plunged ahead. "Um—nice trick with the oars."

His expression didn't change, but after a moment he nodded, very slightly.

We had escaped being swamped, but the struggle to bail out the inrushing waves continued, and for three days I went without real sleep. On the third afternoon, when I finally noticed that the water between the ribs in the hold was only up to my ankle, I was so fatigued that I didn't understand. Then I felt it: the storm-tossed action of the boat had died down.

Zosimea shook my shoulder. "Well, go on, boy, get up on deck!" her voice crackled in my ear. "Tell us what's happening!"

I clambered up the bow hold ladder and looked around. The wind had died, and as I watched, the clouds began to part. In a few minutes we saw our first sunlight in three days. The men began to cheer, but it died out quickly. I could see why. The storm was over, but there was no land to be seen. We were surrounded in all directions by the wine-dark sea.

Lopex crossed the benches to the stern and spoke up.

"Men," he announced, "we've survived the storm, as I said we would. Procoros has tracked exactly where we are. Right now we'll find the quickest route to land, and meet up with the other ships later."

I could see the navigator's angry expression as Lopex approached. I couldn't hear what they were arguing about, but he was gesturing furiously at the sheepskin chart.

I crept closer. "How should I know where we are? And none of this would have happened if we'd made sacrifice!" Procoros was saying.

Lopex had his arms folded across his chest. "The gods help us as they choose, but men are more reliable." He glanced over at me and I busied myself with the bow fire pot. "We had no fresh meat, and no time to organize a hunting party," he continued. "Or do you think that the gods would have been pleased by an offering of dried fish and millet stew?"

Procoros muttered something in which I caught the name *Agamemnon*. Back in Troy, even young children knew that name. The king who had started the war, he was the worst of all the Greek warlords, his name even more hated than Achilles the savage.

"Agamemnon?" Lopex's tone was sour. "I don't believe in that type of sacrifice. Not even with slaves." It would be a long time before I found out what he meant.

All the next day, the men kept one eye over their shoulder as they rowed, waiting eagerly for a glimpse of land. But as the day wore on with the ocean sun beating down on us, the muttering began.

"He doesn't know where we are. We're totally lost," I heard one soldier saying, his voice cracking in the heat. There was a pause for the power stroke.

"Of course he knows," came another voice as they pushed back their oars on the return. "But we can't get back to land. That's why he's not telling us."

"For shame!" A soldier's voice boomed from a few benches away. It was Pharos, said to be the most pious man on the ship. A giant with a billowing black beard, he alone had the wind to speak through the whole rowing cycle. "Live or die in the hands of the gods. Sacrifice and prayer! To mighty Poseidon make your sacrifice, perhaps to spare your lives!"

A few took his advice, clipping locks from their beards and burning them in the stern fire pot during water breaks. What the gods would do with burnt Greek beards, I had no idea. Most, however, preferred just to mutter. The grumbles grew louder on the second day after the storm, when Lopex announced that water rations would be cut to half.

"Half? How can we row on that? Rowing's thirsty work!"

Lopex held up his hand. "No more rowing. The current will take us to shore. We'll stretch the sail over the oars to give us some shade."

By the third day after the storm, the heat was taking its toll on the badly wounded in the rear hold. Despite

Kassander's assurance, I was nervous as I came to report to Lopex. "Sir?" My voice hissed from a dry throat and I tried again. "Sir? One of the wounded men has died. Kyranos."

He glanced sharply at me, but it seemed Kassander had been right. His only comment was, "Keep it quiet, boy, it's bad for morale. We'll deal with it this evening."

After darkness fell, he ordered me to wrap the dead soldier's body in a winding sheet. "Leave it in the hold. Get that beak-faced woman to help you."

The idea of handling a dead barbarian repelled me, but Zosimea plunged in as though he were a pile of laundry, stripping his tunic and sandals to leave the body naked. "Here—sit him up while I wrap this sheet around his shoulders."

Swallowing my disgust, I braced my foot against a cross-strut and pushed him up while Zosimea expertly wrapped his torso, leaving just enough to knot the ends together across his chest. Clearly something she'd done before. We left the corpse in the hold, indistinguishable from the motionless injured men nearby. The next morning it was gone.

I was shocked. An improperly buried corpse had no chance of reaching Hades. I couldn't imagine how the Greeks would react, but Zosimea took it all in stride. "What else can he do, boy? Leave it on board, in this heat? By tomorrow nightfall we'd be jumping overboard ourselves to escape the stink."

She reached into a fold of her threadbare tunic. "Besides,

he'd never have gotten into Hades anyway." She held out the red cabochon that Lopex had given me to put under the corpse's tongue. "No point wasting a good gemstone on a dead barbarian."

We wrapped several more corpses over the next few days, as the injured succumbed to their wounds and the lack of water. Each morning the bodies were gone, splashes in the night. One of the last to go was the old healer, Kallikrates. As I wrapped him in the winding sheet in the airless hold I patted him down for his knife. Someone had already taken it. I shrugged. No honour among these Greek thieves.

By the time Procoros sighted land on the ninth afternoon, a day after our water gave out, his mouth was too dry to shout. But even had he been heard, nobody had the strength to react.

Chapter 11

I WAS DOZING BELOW, my head rolling slightly against one of the hull's wooden ribs as the ship rocked, when I felt the keel grate against pebbles. Down in the hold the sound was louder than on deck, and the other slaves began to wake. Zosimea scratched my shoulder weakly. "Go see," she rasped. Lack of water and the heavy pitch fumes in the hold had left all our throats as dry as fired clay. I rubbed my gummed-up eyes and staggered to my feet.

On deck, a few of the men were starting to sit up. I stood on the hold ladder and squinted out. We had drifted up against a stony shore that led back to steep, shrub-covered hills. There were no other ships in sight. Lopex walked up stiffly and thrust a clutch of goatskin water sacks at me. "Go find water, boy," he said, his voice hoarse. "Find another slave to help. The men can fetch their own after they've had a few mouthfuls."

I stared despairingly at the sacks but went off to beckon Kassander from the hold. As we trudged wearily down the beach, he put a hand on my shoulder. "Lopex is doing you a favour," he said hoarsely. "You get to drink first." A flicker of a smile crossed his cracked lips. "Me too. Thank you."

I hardly had energy to move my feet, but beside me, Kassander seemed to be growing stronger since we'd left the ship, walking with his head up, throwing off his usual crouch. To my relief, we found a trickle of water running across the beach nearby and followed it upstream to its source, a strong spring in a grassy stand of willows. We lay on our stomachs in the lush green grass and put our faces straight into the spring, drinking greedily until we could hold no more. Finally Kassander stirred. "Come on," he said, struggling to his feet. "The men are counting on us."

I looked lazily over at him. "What's your hurry? If the barbarians are thirsty, they can come and get their own."

Kassander hesitated. "Yes. Of course. Barbarians. But they're still human. And don't forget the slaves, they need water too." He shouldered his load and set off. I stood up to follow, shaking my head. Sometimes Kassander was impossible to understand.

The ship was still untethered in the shallows when we

returned. As I reached to climb up the ladder, Kassander stopped me with a touch on the shoulder. "Alexi, find a few more skins and toss them down. I'll go fetch some more water while you serve out what we've got here." I shrugged. Carrying the full skin bags back from the spring was clearly the harder chore.

Lopex had been right. A little water had revived the men enough to get their own, so that afternoon I was sent around to look at their wounds. He had ordered the men who couldn't walk to be laid in the shade of some plane trees at the foot of the hills behind the beach. I knelt beside Pen and unwrapped his bandage. Nine days wrapped in the same filthy rag had done him no good. His leg wound, once healing nicely, now showed a fiery red streak creeping up his thigh toward his heart. I felt a chill. *Eksepsis*.

Pen looked up. Since I'd brought him water that morning he'd been doing better, but his face was haggard. "How am I doing?"

"Uh . . . fine." If their wounds were getting worse, my father never told them. He always managed to sound cheerful. But he had always had medicines. Nobody knew where Kallikrates' medicine chest had gone. From what I'd heard of him, he probably didn't even have one. I thought for a moment. How would my father have treated this?

A breeze from the ocean bobbed the heads of a few straggly red poppies in the grass nearby, stirring a memory. I scrambled up to find Lopex.

He was sitting in his tent, a large pavilion made of sailcloth. The sides were rolled up to let the breeze through, and he was planning repairs with the ship's carpenter.

"Honey?" he said, looking out at me curiously from under his heavy eyebrows. "What do you want it for, boy?"

Ury was perched on a boulder nearby, whetting his sword with a small oilstone. "What stupidity is this, boy? What next—some figs and almonds?"

"Shut up, Ury," Lopex said calmly. "Speak, boy."

"My father used to put honey on wounds that were festering," I replied, feeling awkward. "He said the sweetness drew out the rot."

Behind me, Ury spat on the ground. Lopex shrugged. "Well, boy, if you can find some honey and a volunteer, I'll permit it. But don't expect the soldiers to believe you."

The man in charge of ship's stores was a grotesquely fat one-eared sailor named Demetrios. I found him sprawled on a makeshift bed of purple cloth bolts on the rear deck, a small cloth canopy spread across two oars over his head for shade. Nearby, Zanthos and another sailor were perched on the railing, stitching up rips in the sail.

Demetrios turned his head lazily toward me. "Honey, heh. Not much call for that around here, boy. What do you think we are, the king's palace? What d'you want honey for anyway, hah?"

He'd just argue if I told him. "Lopex wants it."

"Heh." At Lopex's name he heaved his bulky body upright and waddled to the rear hold ladder, leaning on a bronze-tipped cane. I followed him, wondering again how someone so fat was allowed to be part of a group of soldiers.

"Down this way, boy, hah, heh." I couldn't tell whether his strange noises were grunts of exertion or demented chuckles. Following him down the ladder, I watched as he headed for a bulky woollen sack hung from a bronzed nail in a crossbeam. He used a hook on the end of his cane to lift the bag down.

"Yer in luck, boy," he wheezed as he undid the drawstring. "Traded for this with Agamemnon's chief storesmaster just before we shipped. Thought old Odzy might want some for a treat. Picked up a half dozen oars and some sailcloth with it, hah."

He muttered as he fumbled at the knot. "Hera-cursed thing. Anyone'd think he didn't want it opened." His face brightened. "But d'you know what it was we traded him? Our spare mast, heh! Looked sound, but 'twas so rotted out you could break it on your knee. By the time he finds out there'll be a month's water between us."

Grunting in frustration, he pulled out a short knife and sawed through the drawstring. "Here y'go, boy," he said proudly, pulling the bag open. "Honey. Like I says, a good storesmaster can get you anything. Be sure and tell your master." He reached into the bag, and his face changed. "What in Hades—" He snatched his hand out again and dumped the bag on the deck. A musty, dry smell enveloped us as a dozen moths fluttered out. I looked at what he'd poured out. It had once been a honeycomb, but now it was broken into rotten chunks, the wax dark and crumbling, small grubs crawling on the surface. Tangled threads draped like cobwebs across the open combs.

"The gods! Wax moths? That Caractacos! I trusted him, and he trades me wax moths? I hope that mast snaps on his head!" He kicked the pile of rotten comb fragments angrily, scattering them across the floor as several more moths fluttered out, heading deeper into the hold.

He grunted uncomfortably as he bent down to clean up, then glanced at me and straightened again, wheezing. "Well, there she is, boy. Your honeycomb, hah." He gestured at the crumbling mess. "Now pick that up. And make sure you get it all. I like to keep ship's stores tidy."

I looked at the grub-infested mess, dismayed. "But you dumped it out!"

He swung a fat fist at me but I dodged. "You listen to me, boy," he grunted. "I may be fat, but you don't want to find out what kind of trouble I can make for you. Me and old Odz, we go way back. Now clean that up and clear out. I've got some napping to catch up on, heh." He clambered ponderously back up the ladder and I heard his sandals stumping across the deck above me, returning to his shaded corner. Lazy barbarian.

With a sigh of frustration, I started to scoop the scattered bits of moth-infested comb into a pile. I grimaced as my finger poked through a comb cap and sank into a rotten bee larva beneath. When I picked up the bag to put the mess back, it felt heavier than it should. I brought it out into the light. At the bottom of the bag was a cloth-wrapped bundle, tied off with a bit of sailor's ox-hide rope. Inside were another two sections of comb. Unlike the others, they had no strands of moth silk or grubs on the surface. I scratched off a waxy cap and sniffed gingerly. It smelled like honey. Dabbing a bit on my finger, I tasted it. Very sharp, but sweet. I wasn't sure what honey was supposed to taste like, but at least it didn't taste like moth. Well, it would have to do. Silently thanking whoever had packed them separately, I swept the rotten comb fragments into the bag, picked up the cloth bundle and went off to find Pen.

He was propped on his elbow in the grassy shade near the other wounded men. "Hi, Alexi!" he called, waving happily as he spotted me, then glanced around at the nearby Greeks and added gruffly, "I mean, um . . . *you, slave! Come here now!*"

I came over, seething. Why was I bothering to help him? "I'm really sorry," he blurted as I approached. "It's just, they make so much fun of me already. If they knew I was friends with a slave . . ."

"Fine with me," I interrupted, eyeing him coldly. "I don't want them thinking I'm your friend either."

"Oh. Yes. I see," he said uncertainly. His eye fell on the bundle I was carrying. "What's that?"

Suddenly I wished I had never thought of honey, never

fetched it from the ship's stores. I was about to lie, but something in his desperate expression stopped me. Annoyed, I explained what I was planning.

"Um, if you think so, Alexi," he said, watching nervously as I unwrapped the bundle. "But is it," he lowered his voice to a whisper and glanced around, "*safe*?"

What an idiot. "Look, if you don't trust me, I'll just go," I grunted as I scraped the wax caps off a section of comb. "Of course it's safe, it's just honey. What did you think I had here, bees?"

Pen looked embarrassed. Keeping his voice low, he said, "Well, maybe it's different for you Trojans. But the soldiers, they say it's up to the gods if we live or die." Leaning in toward me, he continued in a whisper, "And they really don't like it when you try to change their plans."

I squeezed some honey out and smeared it over his wound. "So what do they expect you to do?"

He swallowed. "Well, we're supposed to wait and see. If the gods want, they'll heal you."

I sat back in disbelief. "Are you *serious*? I always thought we worshipped the same gods. But yours sound as dumb as a whole sack of axes." I tied off his bandage with an angry yank.

Too late, I noticed several soldiers nearby frowning at me, and realized I'd been speaking louder than I'd thought. From behind me came a deep, slow rumble. "Saying what, boy? Thinking our gods be the lesser of yours?"

I stood up and turned around slowly to find myself staring at a hairy navel. Craning my head back, I squinted up into the sunlight until I found his face. It was Pharos, the giant soldier I'd heard advocating sacrifices on board. Slow of thought but as strong as any two men, he was said to practise a muscular devotion to the gods. Around us, several Greeks were drifting over in anticipation.

Unnerved, I reacted without thinking. "*Kopros*, wouldn't anyone?" I snapped. "What sort of gods would tell you not to treat your wounds?"

His expression turned sorrowful. "Gods like not this talk," he said, shaking his head slowly. "Not respectful. Young slave needs to learn respect. Respect for gods!" A hand the size of my head made a sudden grab for me. I darted out of his way, but the soldiers closed ranks to block my escape and a painful kick in my side sent me staggering back. There were chuckles and some jeers. Pen and the other wounded soldiers nearby scrambled out of the way.

Pharos had turned and was heading for me once again. I dodged as he thudded past me, his fingers just brushing my hair. He'd eventually figure out that if he walked slowly, he'd have me. *That tongue of yours is going to get you in a lot of trouble.* Lopex had foreseen this. Why couldn't I control myself? I rolled again to dodge and rose to one knee in the sand to catch my breath, trying to think. Pharos hadn't come looking for me; he had never even spoken to me before. He'd just overheard something I'd said, and then I'd gotten mad and made it worse. Stupid.

Time to change tactics.

Leaping sideways as he thundered past, I called out, "Wait, Pharos! That's not what I meant!" He circled around toward me, and I dodged again.

"I mean, of course we all respect and fear the gods. They control our lives, don't they?" I said, improvising frantically. "But you know the real problem? The gods tell Greeks and Trojans different things!"

Pharos slowed, his head tilting as he scratched his chin through a curly beard as black as Ury's. I glanced around, hoping for inspiration, when my eye fell on the honeycomb, lying in a nearby patch of beach grass. I reached over to pick it up. "Look here! When I talked to Kallikrates about healing, he said he'd never even heard of using honey!" He'd never spoken a word to me, but no one would be asking him anytime soon.

From behind me came impatient catcalls. Pharos stared at me with his arms folded, an impassive gaze that clearly said that a fast tongue could not outrun slow fists. At least he was still listening.

"In Troy, any healer could tell you about it. They—" I caught myself. "I mean, *we* used honey to treat *eksepsis*." I scrambled up onto a rock to get closer to his eye level.

"Pharos, everyone knows you're a man who respects the gods. So I'm sure that of all people, you will know the story of the bees that protected Father Zeus as a child." Inspiration struck. "But in Troy we discovered what he gave the bees in return!"

Lifting the dripping piece of honeycomb above my head, I tried to give my voice the singsong cadence I'd heard from our priests. "In his gratitude, deathless Zeus, king of all the gods, gave their honey the power to *heal*!" I paused to let the murmuring die down, then added loudly, "But only," I paused again, "for those who are truly worthy!"

A buzz of conversation broke out around me. I wiped the sweat from my forehead with my free hand. Pharos was still listening, but a single misstep would break the spell. I chose my next words carefully. "Pharos! They say you are the most devout man in this command. There can be no doubt that immortal Zeus looks on you with favour." I held out the honeycomb toward him. "Let us show the rest of these men together. Permit me to treat your wound with his gift."

Holding my breath, I reached out and gently began to unwrap the filthy bandage around his shoulder. He had refused treatment after Ismaros, and his bandage was ragged and dirty. Quickly, before his ponderous thoughts could crystallize into doubt, I unwound it, wiped out the angry weal beneath and smeared on some honey. Filthy though it was, there was little sign of *eksepsis*. It had a good chance of healing. As I bound him again with a clean bandage from the bag on my waist, I spoke to the watching soldiers, trying to sound confident.

"I believe that divine Zeus will heal this man. Who else here is brave enough to submit their wounds to his mercy?"

There was some uneasy shuffling of feet. "Come!" I called

out, suddenly bold. "Is Pharos the only man here who respects the gods enough to accept their gift?"

After a further pause, someone shuffled forward from the crowd, then two more. Keeping my expression carefully neutral, I unbound their bandages, squeezed the rest of the honey from the comb, and rebound their wounds with fresh cloth.

The comb empty, I stepped down from the rock and walked off toward the circle of men. To my intense relief, they moved aside and let me pass. I took a deep breath, not daring to smile until I was well away.

Later that day Kassander fell into step with me as I was carrying water to the ship's cistern. "Impressive," he commented. "Nice to see your tongue getting you *out* of trouble for a change." I checked my irritated reply as I caught his faint smile.

Chapter 12

THE NEXT MORNING'S sky held a thin layer of hazy cloud, just enough to hide the sun. The men had recovered from their thirst, and a new problem had emerged: food. We were low on stores, and in particular had no more dried meat or fish. Zosimea and I were set to preparing a large pot of porridge over a driftwood fire. As the thick, mealy odour wafted down the beach, the grumbling began. Ury was one of the loudest.

"What's this *kopros*, slave?" he demanded, striding up as I stirred the pot. I'd taken care to stay out of his way since our encounter after Ismaros, but somehow I didn't think he'd forgotten. He snatched the long wooden spoon from me and snarled. "Millet again? This might suit Trojans, but Greek warriors need meat!" He flicked the spoon to splash boiling, sticky porridge across my face. As I yelped and wiped it off, he scooped the spoon into the porridge again. I dodged him and darted off, nearly running into Lopex, who was walking back from the direction of the hills behind the beach.

"Don't like porridge?" he asked. "Good. Then you've both just volunteered for a scouting mission. Along with—" he looked around for a moment and raised his voice. "Pharos. Over here." Pharos lumbered over.

"There's a clean road a few hundred paces back in the hills." He gestured back behind the beach. "And where there's a road, there's a town. Find it. But we're in no condition to raid. Ury, take these two and go visit them. We have plenty of dyed cloth; trade that for food. You can also trade away a dozen tanned cowhides. And there's a box of powders and oils that I took from Troy. Bring that as a sample. Tell them it's powerful Trojan magic that we found in a temple."

I blinked. "It is?"

His gaze flickered to my face. "I don't know what it is, boy, and I don't care. Just trade it for food. Dried meat if you can, fresh otherwise. Also pitch and hide rope. Now get moving. I'm going to start repairs to the ship." He turned back for a moment to look directly at me. "Oh. And get some more honey."

Ury pressed his ugly face close to mine. "I'll see you dead

yet, boy, healer or no. Lopex can't protect you when he's not around. Now stay here while I round up some men."

Pharos swivelled his head to look at him. "Rounding up men? To take only two, Pharos thought."

"Keep your big stupid thoughts to yourself," Ury snapped at him. "I'm not going near an unknown town with only a moron and a slave for backup. Now get your armour on." Pharos said nothing.

A few minutes later, Ury returned with the six swarthy, thick-browed men he spent most of his time with and thrust a heavy wooden box at me, bound closed by tight leather cords. "Carry this, slave." It had a very faint, familiar scent, but I didn't have a chance to examine it before we set off up the hills behind the beach.

Beyond the first line of dusty hills, we found a wide sandy road, lined on either side with small black stones. We were following it through a valley when Ury yanked me back savagely with a hand on my shoulder. "Open your eyes, slave," he hissed in my ear. "Someone's coming!" He waved his men into a stand of trees while he, Pharos and I crouched behind a low tamarisk tree near the road. As we hunkered down, a young woman came down the road, singing to herself. She was slender, her long black hair hanging in a neat plait over a bare shoulder and contrasting with the white dress that brushed the ground as she walked. Her hips swayed as she balanced a cloth bundle on her head; I could hear coarse muttering behind me.

As she came past, I could make out the words of her song. It was a form of Trojan, but with a more liquid, melodic quality. I strained to listen.

Beside me, Ury grunted impatiently. "That's not Greek."

Pharos shook his slow head. "Pharos knows it not."

Ury snorted. "Did I ask you, *gloutos*-breath?" He turned to look at me. "So, boy?" he sneered. "Recognize that?"

I frowned, listening hard. "I think—it's a song about a boy."

Ury reached for his knife. "You understand that yowling?" he said, an unpleasant smile crossing his face. "Pharos, grab her. We'll find out what defences this place has. Maybe we won't be trading with them after all."

Pharos shook his head slowly again. "Must not harm young girls. The gods like it not."

"Oh, for Ares's sake," Ury snarled. "I'll do it."

To my surprise, Pharos grabbed his arm, forcing it down as though it were a kitten's paw. "Not you. The boy. He will talk only. To find out more."

"Let go, you big stupid oaf," Ury growled, struggling, but Pharos's arm didn't budge. Ury grunted in exasperation. "Fine. We'll do it your way. Boy, get out and talk to her. Hurry up, she's getting away."

As I scrambled to my feet he waved his knife at me. "And if you try to run, boy, I'll trench you before you take two steps. Now move!"

I stepped out uncertainly, brushing bracken from my

tunic as she continued down the road away from us. Suddenly I was aware of how long it had been since I'd washed. At least I was wearing a new *chiton*. "Miss? Miss?" I called. "Um. Are you from around here?" Gods, I sounded like an idiot.

Turning around, she saw me and gasped, her hands flying to her mouth and her bundle spilling out across the hard-packed road. "Wait," I called, holding my hands out. "I didn't mean to scare you." I started down the road toward her, palms up in what I hoped was a gesture of friendship.

She glanced expressionlessly at me before bending over to collect the sheets and tunics strewn across the road. As I approached, she scrambled up, giving me a better look at her. About my age, she had a smooth, pale complexion and pretty, doll-like cheekbones. Her eyebrows and long, straight hair were a shiny black. But what I noticed most were her eyes. Almond shaped and exotic, they were carefully outlined with a thin black line. A second glance revealed something else: her pupils were contracted to tiny pinpricks, giving her a disconnected, faraway look.

She said something I couldn't make out, gesturing at the remaining clothing in the roadway, a frown on her face.

"Uh, I'm sorry," I said. I came over and stooped to help pick it up. I must have been doing it badly, because after a moment she giggled and nudged me out of the way. Laying a single white sheet on the ground, she put the rest of the laundry in it and quickly tied it into a loose bundle, then stood up, the bundle balanced on her head. She glanced back over her bare shoulder as she set off down the road. I fell into step beside her.

Gods, this was awkward. This close, her warm, distracting scent filled my nostrils. I scratched the back of my neck, trying to think of something to say. Back in Troy, I'd never spoken much to girls.

"Um. Can I help you carry the laundry?"

She turned her head and looked at me curiously, and I stole a peek out of the corner of my eye. Gods, she was pretty. Her head tipped to one side as she tried to understand. I tried again, aiming for the same liquid quality I'd heard in her song.

Her eyes widened, and she replied. Listening closely, I got it. "Who are you?" she was asking.

"My name's Alexi. I'm from—I'm not from here." My tongue seemed thickened and clumsy, and I changed the topic. "What's your name?"

It took a little while before we could speak without repetition. Her name was Apollonia, from the town of Midhouna, a few minutes away. Down the road the other way, where we were headed, was a river. No, there were no other towns that she knew of nearby; the closest was Han Sghira, about a morning's walk inland. How big was Midhouna? Pretty big, she guessed.

I didn't want to ask, but I couldn't go back to Ury with no

information. "Apollonia?" I said. "Is your town defended? Does it have big walls?"

Her laugh sent a thrill down my back. "Walls? Of course! What else holds up the roofs?"

"No, I mean around the outside. Thick stone walls. For protection."

A pretty frown pursed her lips. "Outside the city? But there are no houses there. Why build walls without houses?"

I tried a different approach. "What about weapons? Do your people have armour? Swords and shields?"

She repeated the words as though she'd never heard them. "Armour? Shields?" She shook her head uncertainly. "I don't know these words, Alexi. Truly, you ask some strange things." Her almond eyes glanced sidelong at me. "But you're very handsome, even if you need a bath. We hardly ever get strangers here." Gods. Trojan girls never spoke this way. At least not to me. I looked away as I felt a blush coming up.

Unaware of the turmoil she was causing, Apollonia casually took out a small white pouch of sticky, dark-brown paste, then expertly pinched off a small piece with one hand and popped it in her mouth. She glanced over. "We call it *ophion*." She smiled at my expression. "We make it from a flower called *lotos*. Would you like some?" she offered, pinching off another small ball of it and rolling it smooth. "Wait. It's better with *sakcharis*." She rolled it in a second pouch of a white, grainy powder. I opened my mouth and she dropped it in.

I chewed experimentally, gagging at the bitter taste that even the sweet white powder couldn't mask. She giggled. "Don't chew. Just swallow. There." She smiled as I choked it down.

"It's not for tasting. For feeling. It makes you feel better. Happier."

We had reached the river, and I scooped some water to rinse my mouth. "Uh, thanks. I guess," I stammered.

"Just wait. You will see." She turned and began to scrub the clothes in the river. As we continued talking, I felt a strange sensation creeping through me, a welling, glowing contentment undermining my thoughts. My memories of my sister were still there, but my feelings were somehow being washed away. I watched Apollonia wringing out the clothes, enjoying her lithe, dreamy movements as she bent to wrap them in a bundle again. She glanced up at my expression and smiled. "It takes us all that way, the first time." She stood up to go, the bundle again balanced on her head, and looked back over her shoulder for me to follow.

As we walked back up the road, I began to feel uneasy, despite the strange calm of the *ophion*. Ury and the soldiers would be hiding by the roadside just ahead. "Let's walk over here," I said, steering her to the other side. She let herself be led, uncomplaining.

"Apollonia," I said quietly, struggling to clear my mental fog. "Does your town have soldiers? Warriors? *Stratiotai*?" I tried all the words I knew, but once again she shrugged her incomprehension.

I grabbed her bare shoulder, trying not to be distracted by the warm touch. "Listen, Apollonia. This is important. You have to tell your people to get ready. There are Greek soldiers near here. I think they're going to raid your town. You have to tell them."

She frowned uncertainly, understanding my tone, but my words weren't getting through. "Go!" I hissed at her. "Danger! Run!" At last, understanding the idea if not the details, she lifted her dress with one hand and ran off around the bend and up the road, her other hand still expertly balancing the laundry on her head.

As I came around the corner, Ury emerged from behind the tamarisk. "What did you say to her, boy?" he growled. "She took off up the road like Hades himself was behind her."

I hadn't thought things out this far. "Uh, she, I mean—" I stammered.

He laughed, a nasty, knowing sound. "Tried to jump her, did you, boy? Tried to drag her into the bushes?"

I blushed, and he smirked. "Couldn't even get that right, eh, boy? Well, did you get anything useful at all? How is the town defended?"

"It doesn't have a wall," I began, wondering how little I could get away with telling him. Not that I knew much. "She didn't understand when I asked her about soldiers or weapons. I think their words must be different. She didn't seem worried about an attack."

Ury chuckled nastily. "So what you're saying is, they're

totally unprepared." He turned toward the stand of fir trees nearby. "Get out of there, you lazy *kopros*-sniffers, we've got a town to raid."

They shambled out sullenly from the trees, grumbling as they approached. I recognized one of them as Theron, his black beard bristling angrily, dark eyes burning. "We've had about enough raiding and looting, thanks very much," he growled. "Thanks to you and Lopex we left a dozen dead back on Ismaros and took twice that in wounds. And if there was going to be an attack, it wouldn't be on your say-so."

Ury rounded on him furiously, cracking him hard on the side of the head with his helmet. "You shut your fat hole, Theron, you don't know what you're talking about. Now get your helmet on, your sandals laced, and your mouth shut. Or would you like to lose a tongue?" he shouted, his hand clutching the pouch at his waist. "The same goes for the rest of you stinking sons of rats. Move!"

The men backed off slowly and began to put on the rest of their armour, shooting surly glances in Ury's direction. We set off down the road, Pharos and me in the lead, Ury driving his men from the rear with a barrage of curses. I wondered whether my warning had got through.

All too soon, the black-lined road spilled out of the valley onto a broad plain, a field of brilliant red poppies along one side and a cluster of low, white buildings in the distance. There was no sign of a wall or even watchtowers. I felt sick. Had I betrayed her?

There was a shout from one of the men. "Soldiers!"

I peered down the road toward the town, relieved, but couldn't quite make them out. They weren't soldiers, I could see that much.

One of the men called out, "Women! They're just *kunai*!"

It was true. Some thirty of them were standing there, spanning the road three deep as though they were waiting for us. The soldiers began to mutter. "Something's not right. They're not afraid of us." Several of the men drew their swords.

We were now close enough to make out details. The women were all wearing pure white dresses that clung to their slender forms, and all had the same high cheekbones and black hair in a queue down their backs. Their faces bore the same calm expression and pinprick pupils I'd seen on Apollonia. I caught a sudden scent.

"Food!" shouted a soldier behind me. The women in the front row were holding out beautiful silver trays, piled high with plump grapes, figs, dates and cheese; others held hot skewers of fragrant roast pork and fish. Behind them were women bearing two-handled *kylices* full of sweet-smelling red wine. And in the rear I could see ornate copper bowls with symmetrical mounds of white-powdered *ophion* in small round balls.

I sniffed the air hungrily, the smell reminding me how long it had been since we'd had real food. Pharos put out his arm to stop me. "Take care," he warned. "Poisoned, this food may be." The men shuffled warily to a halt.

As if they'd understood, each woman shifted her tray to one hand, and in a single graceful motion, pinched off a single morsel of food, slipped it between her lips and swallowed. They picked up another and began to glide toward us.

I held my breath. The men's swords were out and waving warily. But the smell of the food and the perfume of the women were intoxicating. And there was no way they could be hiding weapons.

They slid smoothly up to us, feet hidden by their long dresses, their hips swaying gently as they came on. The men shuffled their feet, muttering, but before their anxiety could tip over into action, the women had slipped wraithlike between the waving swords and were at their elbows, their long, slender fingers slipping morsels into the men's mouths.

A touch on my shoulder. I turned to see Apollonia, a silver tray in her hand, a piece of roast fish in her fingers.

"Apollonia! I was so worried—" I began, but she cut me off gently, slipping the morsel of fish into my mouth.

Gods, it was perfect. Crisp but warm and flaky underneath, seasoned with a hint of cinnamon and a herb I didn't recognize. I ate eagerly, scarcely chewing, only half aware of the men nearby doing the same thing. It was so good my eyes watered. Around me, swords and shields were clattering to the ground as the soldiers lost control, feeding themselves two-handed from the women's silver platters. Behind them, the *kylix*-bearers came on, gently tipping wide vessels of sweet red wine into our mouths.

"Eat, my dove," Apollonia was murmuring in her beautiful liquid speech. Around me were the smooth voices of the other women. "The meat is warm and moist, and the wine is sweet. Eat. Forget."

On an empty stomach, the wine went quickly to my head. I staggered and sat down. My senses dulled, I scarcely noticed when she slipped a heavily-powdered ball of *ophion* between my teeth. A few other soldiers started, alarmed by the bitter taste, but the women's constant liquid warble reassured them and they sat back, delicate fingertips stroking their cheeks.

Soon, a familiar wash of warm contentment was flowing through me. Apollonia offered me another powdered ball, and this time the bitter taste didn't matter. One more, and nothing else did either. I relaxed and let myself be fed.

Hands slipped under my armpits and lifted me gently to my feet. I looked around, dazed. Two women, black-lined eyes and pinprick pupils making them near twins of the others, were tugging me gently toward the nearby town. Apollonia's lips brushed my ear. "Stay here with me, my sweet. Here we have no pain, no sorrow, no memories. Only pleasure, and sweet *ophion*."

I hardly recall being led through the town with the others. We were brought to a house richly draped with fine, red-dyed cloth. There was a soft, soft bed. I slept.

Time drifted past as fog. Waking, eating. More balls of bit-
tersweet *ophion* and deep, dreamless sleep. Apollonia, ap-
pearing like a vision, sweet lips by my ear, soft arms around
my neck. "Soon, my love. Soon you will be one of us. I want
you with us. With me." Content, I waited, tranquil for the
first time in my life. The things that had once so troubled
me—my sister, my father, Troy—were so small. So insignif-
icant. Foolish to have ever let them bother me. A little more
time, and even these musings were gone. And whenever I
opened my eyes, Apollonia was there.

It didn't last. After a time, perhaps many days, there was
commotion in the street outside. Someone in the room. Big,
imposing, angry. I turned my head languidly. Why would
someone wear a metal shirt, I thought vaguely. Feeling myself hoisted onto his shoulder. People in white pulling at him
as he pushed them away. I wondered why. I watched myself
carried through streets, away from town, onto a ship. It
looked oddly familiar, but my mind was full of holes, my
thoughts wriggling away like tiny fish through a net.

Discomfort stirred. Go back. I wanted *ophion*. Apollonia.
Trying to stand up . . . but something was stopping me.
Ropes. Other men tied up beside me. A far-off voice shout-
ing row, curse you, row.

Now the coast was slipping away from us. I tried to say
stop, take me back, but shouting in a dream, my tongue
wouldn't obey. My alarm grew as I began to see what was
happening. Struggling to get loose, I wept with frustration.

Nearby, other men struggled and wept with me as we watched the land of *ophion* recede in our wake.

Bitter as the loss was, the next few days drove it from my mind. That evening, an itch began to well from beneath my skin. The ropes that bound me had some slack, and as the itching grew, I scratched until the blood flowed. But what came next was worse.

The following morning the cramps hit me like a storm wave, pitching me forward and driving my itching skin from my mind. I lay doubled up on the deck, cramped over so far my face was pressed into my knees, my gut twisting like a wrung-out pot rag. Waves of cramp continued to wrack my body, leaving me helpless and writhing on the deck.

On the heels of the cramps came a sudden, wrenching attack of diarrhea. In no time my skin, my tunic, the wooden deck around me were filthy. I was so sick I didn't care, didn't even notice when Zosimea was sent to clean me up and give me water. I didn't care that the rowers could see me, hardly noticed when someone untied my ropes and sat with me.

I'm not sure how long it went on. Two nights, perhaps three. Eventually the cramping attacks began to subside, and I became aware of myself again. My arms and legs were covered with bloody scabs where I'd scratched right through the skin. Despite Zosimea's attention my tunic was soiled, the smell of feces overpowering. Memory of lying doubled up in my own filth in full view of the crew came back as I stood and staggered to the stern rail, avoiding their eyes.

It was the first time on my feet in days, but nobody looked like they wanted to speak to me. Even the normally talkative Zanthos had his head turned away, his nose wrinkled. Too weak to stand properly, I leaned against the rail, watching the bubbles swirl in our wake. Behind me, I could hear some Greeks guffawing as they played *kottabos* across one of the rowing benches.

There was a heavy tread on the deck behind me and a familiar rumble. "Standing at last. My thought, that you might never stand again." Pharos put down a box he was carrying. The rail creaked as he leaned against it. I flicked a silent glance at him. I didn't feel like talking, especially to Greeks.

Behind the ship, a gull screamed and wheeled as it dove for a wriggling fish. I turned my face to let the sea breeze play on my cheeks, gradually blowing the fog from my mind. "Your sickness now is not the *ophion*, but the wanting of it," Pharos added. I looked at him in mild surprise. He added, as though he had read my thoughts, "Pharos speaks, thinks slowly, but deeply too. Most men misjudge him."

A groan caught my attention. Three men were tied to the railing on the port side, looking as filthy and haggard as I felt. Pharos frowned. "Filth, crying in their vomit. With the *lotos*-women, Pharos should have left them."

My blurry memories sharpened and I spoke without thinking. "That was you! You pulled me out!"

Pharos nodded.

"Why?" I said angrily. "Why couldn't you have left me?"

He shook his big head. "Pharos saved you," he said simply.

"Saved me? From what? You think I wanted to come back? To *this*?" I scowled at him. "I was happy there, *Greek*!" Forgetting how weak I was, I let go of the rail and lurched toward him, but staggered and nearly pitched over the railing. He caught me effortlessly and propped me against it.

"Saved you, yes. A healing power the gods have given you, Alexi," he rumbled. "Look." He squatted and slid the bandage off his shoulder where I had treated him a few days earlier. The lips of the wound had joined up, leaving only a fading red line. Despite my anger, I couldn't help reaching over and dragging a fingernail along it. It was smooth and dry, with no sign of *eksepsis*. He nodded.

"The gods favour your Trojan medicine." He bent to pick up the wooden box he had set down and held it out toward me. It was the trade box that we had taken to the village. When I didn't reach for it, he thrust it at me again. Irritated, I unlaced the tight leather ties that held the lid on and peeked in. It was lined with cork-stoppered vials, neatly held in place by leather stays. A mortar and several well-worn grinding *pestilloi* of different sizes were stacked on the bottom, but even with my eyes closed I would have known it by its scent. It was a Trojan healer's box, the vials filled with healing tinctures and herbs. My father had kept one in his *xeneon*.

"For healers." Pharos rumbled. "Yours now, I think."

He set the box down and lumbered back to his bench. I watched him go, thinking angrily of what had been stolen from me. The calm. The contentment. The warm bed. I looked up. *Apollonia*. What had happened to her? Had she tried to hold me there? I concentrated, trying to remember. A pair of dark-lined eyes swam into my mind. A slender, black-haired girl standing to the side, watching calmly as Pharos carried me out, her blank gaze showing no concern, only a mild confusion. I frowned at the thought. A life full of contentment, but empty of passion—was that where the *ophion* had been leading me? I glanced over at Pharos's broad back on his rowing bench. I didn't want to admit it, but perhaps the Greek had saved me from something after all.

Chapter 13

"GREAT ZEUS, WHAT was that?" Beside me on the stern deck, Zanthos gripped his steering oar more tightly. With a gritty crunch, the *Pelagios* had ground to an abrupt halt. A pause, then men's muffled voices in the darkness.

Lopex relayed the words down the ship. "We've grounded on a pebble beach. For tonight, we'll haul the ship up and camp by the water. At first light tomorrow, we'll find out more about where we've landed."

The relief in the voices around me was clear. We'd been sailing blind since the fog had come on us just before dark. The massive cliffs to port had offered no sign of a beaching-point for the night, so Lopex had opted to continue at a slow row rather than drift on the swell.

I awoke early the next morning, lying in the sand to watch the slow dawn light creep like rosy fingers up the hills behind the beach. I missed Apollonia. I missed *ophion*. But if forgetting my life was the price, I didn't want to pay it. I needed to put the island of the *lotos*-eaters from my mind.

The morning was already warm as the rest of the camp began to wake. The previous night's fog was gone, revealing that we had somehow managed to sail blindly up a narrow inlet, guarded by sharp black rocks on either side, to a pebbly beach of dark sand at the end. A short walk up the beach was a stand of poplars concealing a sweet, cold spring. A wooded island lay just off the coast.

Breakfast was millet porridge once again, with a little dried mullet that some of the men had caught and prepared on the beach at Midhouna. The Greeks were passing a *kylix* around, each gulping a mouthful of water from it to rinse their mouths, then spitting it back and passing it on. Barbarians.

I kept a careful eye out for Ury as I stirred the porridge, but I'd seen nothing of him since our encounter with the *lotos*-eaters. If what Pharos had said was true, he was probably too ashamed to show his face.

Over by the *Pelagios*, a loud voice caught my attention. A soldier I didn't know was standing face to face with Lopex, fists on his hips. "*Overboard*? How will we bury him now? How will his shade rest?"

Men's heads turned as the man gestured at Lopex, raising his voice. "Do you know what he's done? Callos, Phota,

Krith—they died of their wounds during the storm after Ismaros. And he threw them into the sea! How can they reach Hades now?"

Angry muttering spread. Even more than the Trojans, the Greeks believed that a proper burial, or for heroes, a cremation, was the only way a soul could reach Hades.

Lopex spun on his heel and jumped to grab the rail of the *Pelagios*, then swung himself up by one hand, muscles flexing. In his other hand he carried a purple mantle which he threw over his shoulders and pinned at his throat with a gold clasp. Dressed like that and standing above us, it was suddenly easy to believe he was a king, back wherever he came from.

He held up his hands for silence. The men ignored him, an angry clamour growing. Mutters broke open into shouts.

"Kritha saved my life at Scamander! This is how he's honoured?"

"What if we die? Will you dump us too?"

Fists appeared clenching swords or knives. This wasn't like Ismaros. This time they weren't ignoring him—they were turning against him.

A flicker of an expression crossed his face, too quick to identify. "That's right!" he shouted, his voice booming above the clamour. "It was hard, but I acted for the living! Do you think they're the first men to die at Poseidon's hand? I sent those poor souls on their way with a gem beneath their tongues valuable enough to buy their passage into Hades ten times over!"

It wasn't working. The men's anger was boiling over now, the crowd beginning to surge toward the ship, carrying me along with it. I scrambled onto a boulder to avoid being trampled.

Lopex spotted me and spoke again. "Wait! You've all witnessed the skill of our Trojan healer. *He* knows the dangers dead men bring." His eye fell upon me. "Isn't that right, boy?"

The men turned toward me on the boulder in their midst, their expressions hard. "Dead men?" I stammered. "What—"

"That's right, boy," he broke in quickly. "Tell them. What you told me. You know. What the Trojan healers knew."

I couldn't think what he was talking about. I opened my mouth, then stopped. Lopex was losing control of his men before my eyes. And Lopex was the only thing protecting me from Ury.

His eyes were fixed on me. I thought fast.

"Dead men? Oh, absolutely. Dead men—" I paused. What would sound convincing? They'd seen a lot more dead men than I had. "Men who die, uh, *over water*, are a danger to everyone around them. You see—" I hesitated, my mind scrambling "—all deaths at sea are the rightful due of Lord Poseidon. For Trojans, this is common knowledge."

I thought for a moment, thankful that none of my fellow Trojans spoke Greek. Lopex was nodding, a glint in his eye urging me on.

"If a body that dies over water, um, isn't returned to his domain soon after death, Poseidon comes for it. He sends spirits. The spirits of—*miasm*. To collect his due." *Miasm*?

Where had that come from? Then I remembered: the old beggar on Armoury Street used to mutter it when people walked by.

I looked at the men as though just realizing something. "You mean—you haven't heard of the *miasm*? Ask Lopex. He knows." Behind the men he was nodding, the corners of his mouth turning up in satisfaction.

"He had no choice. Within"—I chose a number quickly —"two days, at most, they would have been upon us."

Lopex leaned out from the deck of the *Pelagios*, hands chopping out his words. "Heed him, men. With their foul breath, the kiss of the *miasm* takes living and dead alike. Or would you have preferred to taste their breath in your nostrils as you slept? Only by releasing the bodies of our comrades to Poseidon's embrace were we saved."

The men muttered and drew back a pace. I blinked. Just like that, he was back in control.

He straightened up again and let the hard edge of his voice drop. "I know. I want to see Phota and the others safely to Elysium too. So now that our ill fortune is over, I declare a day of celebration! We will send our fallen companions off with a full day of funeral games, feasting, and sacrifice to Lord Poseidon. A celebration that will ensure their passage from Poseidon's realm to Hades!"

The tension in the crowd dissolved and a cheer went up. Lopex basked in it for a moment before turning to climb down the ladder. He brushed past me in the buzzing crowd. "Nice catch, boy," he murmured.

The hunting party that Lopex had arranged returned in the mid-afternoon, bringing the day's funeral games to a halt. Just as well. I'd had enough of watching naked Greeks wrestling and running foot-races in the sand. Even so, if I hadn't been a slave I would have taken them all in the stone throw. After hitting gulls on the wing for supper back in Troy, I could have knocked out their wooden stakes with my eyes shut.

I looked up at the wrong time and caught a gesture from one of the hunters. I sighed and trudged over. Handing me two bare and bloody thigh bones from the carcass on a bronze platter, he trimmed a thick layer of glistening fat from below the skin and wrapped it around them, carefully tucking it around the ends. He pointed to their priest, a thickly-bearded man from another ship preparing a fire on the beach, and gave me a shove.

This had to be a joke. I went to say so but the hunter bent down and clapped a hand over my mouth. "Carry it to the priest, boy," he hissed. "And by the gods, you don't say a single word until the sacrifice is done. Now get going!"

If this was some sort of trick, I wasn't about to play the fledgling for them. As I trotted over to the priest, I joggled the bundle until one edge of the fat slipped off to reveal the bare bones beneath.

The priest's unkempt eyebrows furrowed as he looked at it. "What do you think you've got there, boy? You think the gods will accept *that*?" he whispered hoarsely.

I opened my mouth to reply, but stopped as he began

carefully rewrapping the bundle to hide the bones. As he lanced it with a large skewer and thrust it into the fire, he glanced over at me. "Don't do that again, boy," he muttered. "We can't *ever* let these bones show, or the gods won't accept the sacrifice." As he turned away to waft the smoke into the sky with his free hand, he began a slow chant of offering.

I stared, my mouth hanging open. *That* was a Greek sacrifice? Bones and fat? It was an insult, at least to any gods I knew. But then, whatever the Greeks were doing, it had worked. At least at Troy. I wasn't so sure it was working for them any longer.

The Greeks feasted all afternoon and into the early evening. Long before they could eat all the meat they'd dressed, the strong Ismarian wine had laid them out around the cooking fires, bloated and snoring. We were clustered at one end of the camp near the slaves' fire pit.

Zosimea and I were sitting down to a platter of goat strips that I had liberated from a snoring soldier when a thin, spiteful-looking Trojan woman came up and snatched the plate from me. "Stop! The gods deserve their share. We need an offering of our own. A proper sacrifice, a Trojan sacrifice." Her eye fell upon Kassander lurking by the edge of the camp. "You there! Come here!" Nearby, an unconscious soldier sprawling across a stand of beach grass twitched.

Kassander padded over reluctantly. The thin woman crept up to the soldier and eased his knife from its sheath.

"You're of the age," she said to Kassander. "Do us a proper sacrifice."

He looked down at the knife and shook his head. "I'm sorry," he murmured. "I'm not the right person for this."

"What's the matter, old man?" she said loudly, poking him in the ribs with the handle. "Do you not respect the gods? Perhaps you're an apostate?" She raised her voice and gestured around at the waiting Trojans. "Perhaps it's your fault we're here now!"

Kassander glanced around uncomfortably. "Very well," he said, accepting the knife. He walked over to where the Greeks had draped several skinned goat carcasses across a log. Laying one of them out on a slaughterboard, he knelt and set to work, his back to us. Eventually the woman called out again. "Move it along, old man. These Greeks won't sleep all night."

"I'm nearly done. The light is poor." A moment later he scrambled to his feet, holding the board in both hands. "Here," he said awkwardly.

There was a murmur from the waiting slaves. This wasn't right. In the twilight I could just make out two long bundles on the board, wrapped in glistening sheets of fat. The thin woman stalked over and picked one up. "What are you playing at, old fool?" It slipped from her hand, exposing two bloody foreleg bones that tumbled to the ground.

The watching Trojans gasped. The woman picked up one of the bones and shook it at him. "What is this?" she hissed.

"Are you trying to insult the gods?" It looked just like the Greek sacrifice from earlier in the day.

Kassander took an uneasy breath. "I'm sorry. I haven't done this in a long time." His eye fell upon me. "Alexi! Can you come and lend me a hand?" he said anxiously, his accent stronger than usual.

As if a torch had been lit, I suddenly saw the pattern. His accent. How he knew so much about Greek customs. How he hid his face around the Greeks. And how he didn't know something any Trojan boy could have told him—what a Trojan sacrifice looked like.

"Wait," I breathed, staring at him. "You're not Trojan at all." My eyes opened wide. "You're Greek!" He looked over at me uncertainly. "That's it, isn't it?" I said. "You're one of them!" A soldier beyond the fire mumbled something and rolled over at the noise.

Kassander dropped the board and swept over to me in a few quick strides. "Alexi," he said quietly. "Please."

"Why should I help you, Greek?" I spat. Dismay flickered across his face.

"Keep it quiet, Alexi," he murmured, glancing at the sleeping soldiers nearby. "You don't know how dangerous this is."

"Dangerous?" I shot back. I was so angry I was shaking. "You attacked us! How many Trojans did you kill, Greek?" The soldier in the beach grass nearby stirred and caught my eye. "Maybe I'll wake him up and ask! Hey! You!" I called. "Did—" but my voice was choked off as Kassander's hand clamped over my mouth. He put his face down to mine.

"Alexi, please. I swear I have good reasons for what I've done. If I promise to tell you everything, will you agree to stay quiet and help me with the sacrifice?" I struggled for a moment, but he was much stronger than he looked. Eventually, I nodded.

He took his hand away tentatively, then straightened up. "My apologies, everyone," he said to the Trojans, who had been watching our exchange curiously. "Just a misunderstanding. We'll have a sacrifice ready shortly." He took my arm and guided me over to the dying fire where he had prepared the first one. Laying out another goat, he knelt beside it and looked up. "Okay, Alexi. What does a Trojan sacrifice?"

I shook my head. "You first."

Kassander sighed and tapped the ground beside him. "Sit down, Alexi. I said I'd tell you."

I stayed standing, my arms folded. "So tell me." Then I frowned. He'd answered in Greek! He caught my eye and nodded.

"That's right, Alexi. I'm Greek. They don't know it's me. I need to keep it that way."

"Why?"

"Please, Alexi," he said. "Kneel here and help. I'll explain as we work. What parts do I need?"

I took a breath and knelt beside him. "First the heart. Now start talking."

He set methodically to work cracking the breastbone. "My real name is Arkadios," he said. "I was a commander in the Greek army, a *lawagete*."

"You were a general?"

He nodded. "Close." The chest cavity was open now and he was feeling inside expertly with the tip of his knife. He glanced over. "Commanders have to take the omens before a battle. I've eviscerated a few beasts in my time." His hand came out, dark with cold blood, holding the heart. "What else do I need?"

"The liver. If it's a special occasion, a lung as well."

He looked up at me. "Is that all?"

"Were you a spy?"

Kassander shook his head and bent back over the carcass. "We were losing the war, Alexi. We weren't prepared for an operation this long. King Agamemnon thought you Trojans would welcome us! Liberators from the tyranny of your King Priam." He paused to scratch his nose with the butt of the knife.

"We were too far from home, with no supply lines. We spent more time raiding down the coast for food than we did fighting. By year three we were down to two meals a day, and meat once a week." He removed the liver and laid it beside the heart.

"You think it was better for us?" I said. "We were starving! And you started it, Greek."

He sighed. "I'm not looking for sympathy, Alexi." He began sawing at something in the chest cavity. "It had become clear we would never win," he continued. "My general agreed, but when he spoke of it, Agamemnon had him killed outright. Conditions were terrible. By mid-winter of year five the only meat available was rats. And still Agamemnon refused to admit defeat."

"You started it, Greek," I repeated. Anger was making my tongue thick. "You could have stopped it."

Kassander looked up at me. "I'm sorry we brought this on your people. And I'm sorry I couldn't be honest with you."

"You've been lying from the day we met!" I broke in. "Why should I believe you now?"

Kassander sighed. "I've been honest about everything except who I was. I couldn't tell anyone that." He rubbed his hands, slippery with goat blood, in the sand beside his knees, then dusted them off and picked up the knife again. "You see, Alexi, the Greeks don't take kindly to traitors."

"Traitors?"

"It was the plague in the ninth year that finally tipped the scales for me. It hit our whole encampment hard. Men walking around healthy one day were dead two days later. My unit was one of the hardest hit."

He pulled a neatly separated lung from the chest cavity and laid it beside the heart and liver on the board. "What else do I need?"

I gestured impatiently. "Go on."

"The seers said it was because Agamemnon had insulted

Apollo by taking a priestess as his slave." He shrugged. "I don't know, but when he refused to admit it, the entire Myrmidon army dropped arms and withdrew from the war. That was the moment I realized we were all going to die there. Agamemnon would never withdraw until the last of us was dead. With my unit destroyed and my commanding officer killed, something inside me snapped." He took a deep breath. "That night I crept out of camp and knocked at the east gate. Your King Priam confined me to a wing of the palace, something between guest and a prisoner. When the Greeks came, it was a simple matter to dirty my face, dress as a slave and let myself be captured."

"You're lying." I could feel my blood rising again. "Back at Ismaros you said the Greeks would kill anyone who could be a soldier in disguise. So why didn't the Greeks kill you?"

"I was telling the truth, Alexi," he said quietly. "The trick is to act so much like a slave that they never even think of you as anything else. Stoop. Cringe. Keep your eyes dull. Most importantly, never look them in the eye. I've been doing it since Troy. You'd do well to learn how."

I glanced back to see the same spiteful-looking woman stalking toward us, and reached to unfold the lung and arrange the liver and heart as I'd seen the priests do. "Is there something I need to say?" he muttered.

"Apollo Protector and Life-Giver Helios, thanks and praise," I muttered back. He scrambled up, board in hand, and turned toward the slaves.

"Above your head," I hissed. He hoisted the board over his head without a pause and repeated the consecration. The slaves filed forward one by one to touch the edge of the platter, then headed quickly for the now-roaring slaves' fire to fill their bellies.

Kassander stood until they had all gone by, then at my instruction led the way to a high boulder. He set the board down on the rock and turned to me. "We're not that different, Alexi," he said softly as we gathered kindling to burn the offering. "We're both slaves of the Greeks. And we each have a secret."

My gaze snapped in his direction. "What do you mean?"

His voice developed a sudden hard edge. "I've told you this because I need your help to stay hidden, Alexi. If you're ever tempted to give me up to the Greeks, just remember that I'm keeping your secret too." His hand clamped my elbow in a grip like a blacksmith's tongs, and he looked me hard in the eye. "I know who killed Ury's brother."

Chapter 14

THE CAVE GAPED out of the hillside like a mouth. Before it, a semi-circle of boulders jutted to create a large, sloping courtyard. A high awning of rough timber shaded the entrance from the mid-afternoon sun. It could have been any shepherd's cave from the hills around Troy, except for one thing: it was far too *large*.

We had spotted the cave that morning while exploring a small offshore island in the *Pelagios*. Lopex had left the other ships at the larger island we had landed on two nights earlier, with orders to refit and provision.

Upon sighting the cave, Lopex had insisted that we return to the ship, beached at the eastern tip of the island, to fetch more of the wine he had taken at Ismaros. There were twelve of us with him, leaving the rest of the crew with the *Pelagios*. Ury was one of the twelve.

We watched for a few moments, but nobody was moving near the cave, the tangled thicket of grapevines on the hillside unattended. "Come on, men," Lopex called. "Let's see who lives here." He strode off up the hill, his purple cloak billowing behind him.

Except for the sword across Lopex's back, the weapons had been left at the ship. "By making alliance with our enemies the Trojans, the Cicones made us their enemies. Whoever these people are, they did not. Our duty to Zeus, patron of guests, demands that we approach them first in peace," he explained as we set off.

The hillside below the entrance was strewn with rubble as if its inhabitants had heaved huge boulders out of the cave like shot-put stones. As we picked our way around them, the soldiers griped at the weight of the wine skins, but Lopex overruled them. "To arrive empty-handed would be an insult. Noble families exchange guest-gifts as a gesture of respect."

"Good for them, Lopex, but what does it do for us?" grunted a wiry, sharp-nosed soldier, pausing with his foot on a boulder. It was Deklah, one of the two men who had carried Ury's brother back to the camp outside Troy. Beside him, the other men took the chance to rest, putting down their loads.

Lopex turned. "What it gives you, Deklah, is honour. The honour of *xenios*, of the gift-giver. Just as it will honour the people who live here."

There was a sudden flapping of wings from up the hill. Startled by our approach, a white partridge had taken flight from the scrub bushes near the cave. Lopex spun on his heel and pointed to it, shielding his eyes from the sun as it flew over our heads. "Mark you, men. Did you see where that bird flew from?" He pointed up the hill. "There. The *right* side of the cave. Can anyone doubt this omen of luck from immortal Zeus?"

He *had* to be kidding. My grandmother used to reminisce about it, but nobody who still had their own teeth believed in bird flight augury any more. Did they? To my amazement, the Greek soldiers were nodding. Even Pharos was rumbling his approval. Lopex's lips twitched in a quick half-smile, and I wondered again whether he believed anything he said.

All the same, as the men started up the hill again, I heard Deklah muttering to himself as he passed. "That's great. Let's just hope it's an omen for us, not them."

From up close, the cave looked more than ever like a mouth, the half-circle of stones an out-thrust jaw. A huge, mossy boulder stood guard beside the entrance. I walked in reluctantly behind the others and waited for my eyes to adjust, nerves fluttering uneasily in my stomach. But if I'd known what was to come, I would have been screaming.

"Sweet Apollo!" someone muttered. The mouth was big,

but the cave inside was enormous, its ceiling so high that our footsteps echoed on the rock floor. Around us, food lay in every direction. Circles of cheese as big as cartwheels lay in heaps along one wall. Farther in, stacks of huge baskets overflowed with grapes the size of hen's eggs, the bunches still trailing ragged lengths of vine. Deeper along the left wall a herd of young goats were corralled, while high overhead, smoked goat and mutton hung in clusters like giant bats from beams below the cave ceiling. Overlaying everything was the persistent, throat-catching smell of sheep dung.

"By the name! Look at all this food! You know, just how many men live here?" came Deklah's voice.

"And how do they get *those* down?" someone else wondered, eyeing the dangling carcasses. I glanced up. The beams were far too high to reach, even with a ladder.

"Come on," another soldier said urgently. "They're all out. Let's grab what we can carry and get away before they come back."

Lopex had ventured a little deeper. He held up his hand, his back to us. "We are warriors. Not house thieves. We will wait for the people who live here."

The men looked at each other. "But Lopex," began Deklah, "what if they're not so friendly? You know, not everybody we meet is all honey breath and sweetbreads." There were mutters of agreement.

Lopex turned and walked back to them. "Are you the men who ravaged Troy? Or a mudhole of croaking frogs?" The men shuffled awkwardly as he walked past them, staring into each man's eyes in turn. "If you steal now, you dishonour Zeus's augury to us. We wait."

Although he wouldn't let them steal, he consented to their eating some of the massive store of food, so long as they made sacrifice first. How that was different I couldn't see, but with this much food I doubted anyone would notice. Encouraged, several soldiers began hacking chunks from the giant slabs of cheese, while others slaughtered three young kids from the pen. The cave roof was so high that the smoke from their cooking fire disappeared above us.

Once again, what they sacrificed to the gods was a bundle of thigh bones hidden in fat, keeping the meat and internal organs for themselves. More proof, it seemed to me, that their gods weren't that bright. But it wasn't up to me to tell them they were getting the smelly end of the fish.

As always, I was hungry, and the smell of roasting goat was so good it made me itch. I squatted against the rough rock wall as I waited, trying to ignore that maddening odour. Looking around for a ladder or pole that might reach the hanging meat, my gaze stopped at a shallow crevice in the wall. The late afternoon sun didn't reach it, but it was now fitfully lit by the flickering fire. Something inside caught my eye.

It was a piece of flattened bronze standing on end, a little taller than a man and battered into a crescent. The curved outer edge showed the scratches of periodic sharpening, while the inner edge was lined with a thick piece of well-worn, dark wood. If it weren't so large, it would look almost like—I rubbed my eyes, stinging from the smoke, and looked again, a knot forming in my stomach.

Nearby, Lopex was chewing on a haunch of roast goat, his foot on a rounded stone. "What are you looking at, boy?" he asked.

I pointed, and Lopex glanced up. Suddenly his eyes narrowed and he peered hard for a moment, then straightened and stepped up on the stone.

"To me, men!" he called out. "Drop what you're doing. We're leaving *right now*. The people who live here are not what we think. In fact—"

A noise came from the mouth of the cavern. Something was blocking the setting sun. Something large.

Momentarily in shadow, we reacted as one, darting farther into the cave and ducking behind a huge boulder. As a slave and the smallest, I was pushed to the edge. Half exposed, I could see something huge crawling in through the cave entrance.

A low rumbling came from it. It took me a moment to recognize it as speech, a strange, knotted form of Greek. "In cave, who?" it rumbled to itself, bending down to peer at the Greeks' cooking fire. "Eaten goats, somebody."

"Sweet Apollo," someone muttered. "What is it?"

No one had an answer. We watched as the giant creature stood up inside the cave mouth and ushered a huge herd of sheep and goats inside. It turned and ponderously pulled the massive boulder across the entranceway, sealing it closed.

The thing bent down to blow on the embers of our cooking fire, then threw what looked like a small tree into the pit. As it flared, we saw the creature's face for the first time.

It was hideous. A thick, slab-sided head squatted atop its massive shoulders like the peak of a mountain. At the centre of its forehead, a solitary eye peered out from a bony socket like some brooding cave animal. Below it swelled a clay-lump nose pierced by a ragged nostril, from which something yellow trickled into a lipless mouth. A name surfaced from my grandmother's stories: *Cyclops*. The wheel-eyed monster.

Several men gasped and began to mutter prayers. The noise caught the creature's attention and it scrambled to its feet. Even crouched beneath that huge ceiling, it was as tall as an oak.

"Ah ha!" it growled, stumping closer as we cringed against the wall. "Thieves in cave, see you now!" It bent down to peer at us, its broad belly spilling over the edge of its crude loincloth. "Eat my goats? Now eat you!" Its hands shot out and grabbed the two soldiers on either side of me like children's dolls.

We watched in horror as the creature smashed their heads against the wall of the cave and dropped their bodies onto a stone ledge high above us. Seizing the crescent knife I'd spotted earlier, it began hacking the bodies into grisly chunks. Gobbets of flesh and fragments of bone rained down to spatter the cave floor around us. The creature ate them raw, its massive teeth crunching through their bones like pine nuts to leave only their heads. Finished, it washed the meal down with noisy gulps of water from a huge urn near the door before wiping its hands on its filthy loincloth. A shattered head rolled from the ledge and clattered to the stone floor nearby to stare up at us with its remaining eyeball.

I felt sick. Behind me, men were retching. The thing looked up from its gruesome meal, the skin around its lipless mouth bloody. "Again I ask, give your name!"

I watched in astonishment as Lopex stepped out from behind the rock and strode boldly up to it. No one could doubt his courage. As he approached from the side, he paused for a moment, then waved one arm. The beast took no notice. Lopex moved closer and waved again. Once more there was no reaction. I couldn't imagine what he was doing—did he *want* the thing to eat him?

Finally he spoke, his hands cupped around his mouth. The creature's head jerked around.

"We are Achaeans, destroyers of the city of Troy. The gods chose to blow us off course and bring us to your island. We came to your cave to exchange such guest-gifts with you as civilized men do. But it is clear that you are a stranger to such customs. Beware, O Cyclops. All-powerful Zeus, who avenges the ill-treatment of travellers, even now has his eye fixed upon you. Let us go free, and he may yet spare you."

The creature stared at him and belched, a rumbling, rolling sound that filled the air around him with the smell of raw flesh, then bent to reply.

"Gods on high I heed not, even less the laws of men. But if tell what I ask, gift-of-guest I will give, even so."

Lopex folded his arms. "Ask, then."

"Came you how, thief of goats? Your ship, where? And your name, what be called?"

Lopex didn't hesitate. "We arrived by sea, returning from a heroic war with the city of Troy. Because of us, the crows now feast where the palace of Priam once stood.

"As for our ship, it is lost. The rocks that guard the western end of your island ground it to dust when we chanced upon them in the fog two nights ago." As always, the lies came to him as naturally as breathing.

The Cyclops grunted and seemed to think for a moment, holding up first one finger, then two, frowning at them. "Answers two," it growled at him. "Where is last? Tell your name."

This time Lopex hesitated for an instant. "Very well. I will give you my name." He paused again. "My name, O Cyclops—is Nobah. Nobah, of the venerable Achaean family of—Djee. Now, I have answered your three questions. Deliver your gift."

The creature put its lipless mouth down near my master's face and whispered, a stentorian rumble that carried through the cave.

"Gift-of-guest, Nobah Djee? This it is, yours alone. Feast shall I, on your men. Trap in cave, two by two. But of you, I eat last. This I give, as gift-of-guest." Its laugh was a hot blast of sound. Lopex staggered backwards as a mast-thick finger jabbed him in the chest.

Chapter 15

ONLY LOPEX SLEPT that night, as the snores of that massive thing thundered through the cave like an avalanche. I spent a restless night on the stone floor until the narrow rays of morning light slipping around the boulder at the cave mouth roused the creature.

As it unfolded its massive limbs and stood up, I scuttled for the back of the cave along with the others, but this morning it was paying us no attention. Snatching up one of its cartwheel-sized cheeses, it sat down across from the stock pens to gnaw on it. Lopex spoke up, keeping his voice low.

"Now listen, all of you. That creature is a Cyclops. As you've seen, they're big and strong, but not smart, and they eat anything. But all creatures beneath the gods have a weakness. Even mighty Achilles, as we saw before the gates of Troy." He paused and nodded toward the beast, now finished its meal and waddling toward the stock pens. "The Cyclops will have to let its flocks out to graze. I want two squads, one beside the corral and the other on the far side by that large urn. When it rolls the stone away, choose your time and run in twos as the flocks are going out. Last night I showed you that it can see only what is directly in front of it. Stick to the edges of the cave mouth and it won't see you. Once you're outside, split up and find cover. Now move!"

Keeping my distance from Ury, I followed Lopex, slipping into his group as they took position behind a large urn.

We had expected the creature to push the entrance wide open as it had last night, but it was smarter than Lopex thought. This morning, it heaved the boulder aside just far enough to create a narrow gap. The sudden light made me wince, and I squinted, dismayed, as I watched the creature kneel beside the entrance, scrutinizing the jostling beasts one by one as they trotted out. There was no way we could escape without being spotted now.

The creature stood up to follow its flocks out, but turned back to face our way for a moment. "Cheese in morning. Hungrier tonight," it grunted. "Eat well, thieves in cave." It turned and squeezed through the gap, rolling the huge stone closed behind it.

Sealed again into the tomb-like darkness, some of the

men began to whimper. "Gods, now what do we do? We're all going to die here!" Other voices were rising. "What did we come here for anyway? This is all Lopex's fault!"

Sitting on a rock spattered with scraps of brain, Lopex seemed lost in thought. After some time, he stood up. Bits of gore stuck to the back of his purple cloak.

"Listen here, men," he said. "The Cyclops will be back tonight with its flocks. We can't kill it. That boulder is too big for us to move by ourselves and we can't dig around it, the cave mouth is solid rock. We must even our chances. If you do what I say, we can get out safely."

"It's going to come back and eat us, and you're just sitting around!" Deklah's voice carried a note of hysteria. "Plans? By the Name, we might as well make plans against an earthquake! Maybe we should give you to it for getting us into this!"

Lopex's bright sword was at Deklah's throat so fast I didn't even see it move, the edge pressing a deep furrow into Deklah's skin. Unlike most of their weapons, it was shiny, uncorroded—and very sharp.

"Is that really the path you want to go down, Deklah?" Lopex asked softly. "If being eaten alive is your fear, I can solve that for you right now." He paused. "Or would you prefer to listen?"

Deklah said nothing. It looked like he was trying to nod without moving his neck. Lopex lowered his sword.

"Right. It's very simple." His eyes narrowed as he looked

around at the men. "When that thing comes back tonight, we're going to blind it."

We spent the rest of the morning getting ready. Searching in the gloom, Lopex uncovered a long, straight piece of dark olive wood in a timber heap near the animal pens and hacked off a ten-pace length with his sword. After carving a tapered point at one end, we buried it under the straw again.

"Even blind, the Cyclops will have to open the cave to let its flocks out," Lopex explained. "When it does, we can easily escape without being spotted. So once it's asleep tonight, we will heat the end of our stake in the fire and stab it through the eye."

"But Lopex, what if it wakes up before we stab it?" came a tremulous question.

Lopex glanced over. "Leave that to me."

With the stake ready, I crept off quietly before Ury could spot me and settled down behind a pile of half-rotted cross-posts. Back here, the pleasant scent of mouldering wood almost overcame the ever-present smell of dung, and I lay back, wriggling my shoulders against the gravel. A black cave ant struggled to drag a fleshy lump to its nest in the woodpile.

I'd tried to pretend I didn't understand when Kassander had told me he knew who Ury was looking for, but he'd just shaken his head. "You haven't been careful enough to hide your limp, especially when you're tired. And it was clear

Deklah and Takis were lying about the great warrior that killed Brillicos the night Troy fell. That, and a few things you've said about your sister."

I began a denial but he brushed it aside. "Look, Alexi. I'm not going to expose you. You did us all a favour—Ury is brutal, but his brother was brutal *and* bright. Just be careful what you say about your sister. As a fellow slave, I know you a lot better than the Greeks, but if I can make these connections, others may too. And as you love life, *don't limp.*"

Beyond the woodpile, several of Ury's scowling cronies had fallen to arguing. Knives flashed in the narrow sunbeams that squeezed past the boulder. There was a furious shout and something shiny came spinning my way to sink point-first into a rotting log beside me. I reached over to throw it back, but my attention was caught by the engraving on the handle.

I stared at it, caught in a sudden wash of memory. Someone seemed to be shouting from a long way off. As I stared at the dagger, the image of Mela's crumpled body overwhelmed me. My heart raced as the memory of that night closed in on me again.

Suddenly two hulking soldiers were looking down at me. "Are you deaf or just stupid, boy? I said hand it over," one growled, snatching the knife away. Pinned by my insistent memories, I couldn't answer. He gave me a vicious kick in the ribs and both soldiers walked away, shaking their heads.

This time the spell didn't last as long. As I came back to

the present, I scrambled over the pile of logs without thinking. "That dagger—where did you get it?"

The soldier who had taken it turned around. It was Sophronios, one of Ury's accomplices, a scowling man with a livid slash across his broad nose. "What do you care, slave boy?" When I didn't answer, he shrugged. "Took it off some Trojan bint. By some steps."

Someone made a brief, choked-off noise. The soldier looked down at me, a nasty smile creasing his ugly face. "Someone you knew, was she?"

My expression must have answered, because he glanced over at the other soldier and winked. His smile broadened as his fingers stroked the gash on his nose. "Well now, isn't that a funny thing, me talking to you about her. I have some bad news about your girlfriend, slave boy. Don't plan on ever talking to her again. Know why?"

I stood frozen, desperately willing myself not to hear, but his words pushed their way in like a spear point. "Because after I cut her throat she couldn't talk no more!" He let out a roar of laughter, digging his companion in the ribs.

I took an involuntary step toward him, not even sure what I was planning, but the flash of the knife point before my face stopped me. "One more step, slave boy. Just one more," he breathed.

Despite the rage flooding through me, I managed to stay silent. The two men walked away, laughing, and after a long moment I turned and crept back to the woodpile. I had recognized that knife by the engraving of the goddess Artemis on the handle. It had been my father's coming-of-age gift to Melantha, the day she turned thirteen.

The noise of the boulder being pushed aside awoke me, and I bolted for the darkness of the back of the cave with the Greeks. The creature let its flocks in and pulled the boulder shut, then sniffed the air carefully and lumbered toward us. "Hungrier in evening," it grunted. "Hungrier now."

Caught in the front row, I squirmed as its massive head swivelled on its shoulders, aiming its eye at us one by one before stopping on me.

Two powerful hands clamped onto my shoulder from behind me as Sophronios's voice hissed in my ear. "You just stay put, boy. I knew Ury had kept you around for a reason." I twisted frantically to escape that deep-set eye, but Sophronios held me pinned before him.

One of the creature's flabby hands reached for me in the gloom. In desperation, I lunged straight up against the hands on my shoulders, then as Sophronios was briefly off balance, I slipped out of his grip to drop like a dead weight to the stone floor.

The huge hand shot over me to snatch up the crouching Sophronios instead. As the creature hoisted him high into the air, he shrieked and gibbered like a man insane.

"Wait," he cried out. "I'm not the one you wanted! It's the

slave! Take the slave! Oh, sweet gods, please, no! No!" His voice rose to a high-pitched shriek, abruptly cut off with a horrible liquid crunch as the Cyclops smashed his head against the rock wall above us. His skull shattered, spattering us with gore. In the dim light I caught a momentary glimpse of a soldier in the creature's other hand, his eyes closed, mouth moving in what must have been a prayer, until it was cut short the same brutal way. Then came the quick sounds of knife against bone, knife against stone, and the grisly crunching, chewing noises of the night before.

The men muttered in shock and anger, and I closed my eyes quickly. "Did you see that?" came Ury's growl. "That snivelling slave ducked so that thing would grab Sophro instead. Get up, you stinking coward." A bronze-shod sandal kicked me in the ribs, and I struggled to appear unconscious.

Then came another voice. "Kick him not. He has fainted, I think." Someone lifted my head and started gently slapping my cheeks. I let my eyes wobble open to see Pharos on one knee beside me. "Not to blame you for fainting," he rumbled. "But stand now, before the kicking begins once more."

I stood up shakily. After what I'd just seen, my wobbliness was no act. "Oh, gods," I said, trying to sound dazed. "What happened? That huge hand, it . . . was coming right for me." I frowned and looked around as if realizing something. From off to the side, Lopex was watching me closely.

I pretended not to notice. "What—why am I still here?"

"You fainted, you worthless *koprolith*, and that thing took a better man because of you," came Ury's snarl. "I should kill you now and leave you out for a snack."

Lopex spoke up, keeping his voice low. "Drop it, Ury. It could have been any of us. Now get ready, all of you. It's time."

Fetching two tan wineskins from behind a boulder, he strode out of the gloom to where the creature was finishing its grisly meal by the fire. I watched, as astonished as the first time.

"Ho, Cyclops!" he called. The creature stopped and turned its head toward him, a bloody, sandalled foot sticking out of its lipless mouth. I gagged.

"Any flesh goes down more smoothly with a cooling draught of wine," he continued.

The creature looked at him suspiciously. "*Wine*, what is?" it grunted. "I know it not."

Lopex unshouldered one of the wine skins. "I had brought these as a guest-gift. But now I must offer it to you in the hope that you will spare us." He unlaced the mouth and held the skin up.

The creature snatched it. "Spare you not," it growled. "But slow my hunger it may, if I like." The creature opened its mouth when a frown creased its face. "Not to drink this gift-of-guest. To poison me, your plan must be."

Lopex eyed the creature, hands on his hips. "If poisoning

you would further my ends, I would do it in an instant," he replied. "But if you died here we would die with you, for all of my men together could not budge the boulder that seals us into your cave. If you disbelieve, let me drink some."

The creature grunted and sprayed some wine from the skin into my master's mouth, splashing his face and tunic a dark red. Waiting for a few moments until it was satisfied, it raised the skin to its own mouth and shot a stream of wine into the back of its throat.

It coughed momentarily, then recovered and squeezed the skin empty. Letting it fall into its lap, the creature growled, "Strong in mouth but good, this *wine*. Bring me more, or feast I shall upon your men."

Lopex gestured for another skin and held it up. After several more, its speech had become slurred, but Lopex gave it no chance to think. "Creature!" he called, holding up yet another. "Drink! Do you not find the taste improves with each draught! Quickly, quickly! Drink!"

With each new skinful its massive hands grew clumsier, its balance poorer. As Lopex handed it yet another, I could see it wobbling where it sat. Frowning stupidly at the skin in its hand for a moment, it opened its mouth, but its huge fleshy eyelid flickered and slid shut. The wine skin slipped from its fingers, and the creature keeled slowly over to sprawl on the cave floor, its cheek to the ground. The cave filled with its snores.

Lopex watched until it was soundly asleep, then turned to

us. "I thought so," he said, sounding pleased. "Look around. No grape presses. No fermentation pots. It's never had true wine before. Six full skins should put that brute out until morning."

The creature was sprawled on its back, its head facing our way, one flabby cheek pressed against the rock floor, its eye within easy reach. The men stoked the fire to prepare the stake, turning the point over and over in the flames until it was hard and hissing hot. But as the four men holding it took position in front of its face, the creature stirred. The men froze.

With an odd, high-pitched snort, it smacked its lips, rolled slightly and subsided on its back, its head now propped up against the cave wall. A trickle of drool seeped from the corner of its mouth and ran down its neck.

There was an anxious murmur from the men. "Now what will we do?" came Deklah's plaintive whisper. "It's too far! We can't reach the eye any more!"

Lopex frowned for a moment. "The plan will still work. You'll just have to thrust high, over the chest."

Deklah stared at him, wild-eyed. "That's your plan? What do we look like, Titans? How will we aim? It's too far away!"

Lopex looked around. "I made the stake long enough for this. We just need someone to climb up on the chest to guide our aim. Someone light enough that it won't wake." His eye fell on me behind the woodpile, now illuminated by the blazing fire. "Boy! Come out here!"

I climbed out slowly. He picked up an unburnt branch from the fire and hacked at it with his sword, leaving a long forked stick. "Here's where you come in, boy. Take this and climb up on that thing's chest. You're going to steer the stake into its eye."

I looked up at the sleeping creature and quailed. Approach those hands—and that huge mouth? I looked around desperately as Lopex grabbed my shoulder.

"Don't worry. With that much wine inside him, he won't wake up. And you'll just be up there for a few moments." His grip tightened as he leaned down and added, "And if you won't do it, you're no use to me anyway."

I swallowed and looked up at the Cyclops. It chose that moment to twitch one of its flabby arms, and I leapt back. It didn't move again, and I crept closer. From here, it was even bigger than I'd realized. Its chest was as thick as I was tall. I gulped, wondering how to climb up.

"Put your foot here." Lopex bent beside me, his fingers laced to make a step. I put in one foot, and he immediately gave a powerful heave that threw me up onto the creature's chest. The Cyclops grunted and I froze, but it just smacked its huge lips again and lapsed back into its stupor. I waited to see if it would move again.

Lopex hissed at me from the cave floor. "What are you doing, boy? Get going!" Trying to be as light as possible, I began to creep up its chest on my hands and knees as hot puffs of putrid breath washed over me. Ahead, sheets of snot flapped in a wormhole nostril big enough to put my fist in. I climbed gingerly to my feet and held the forked stick up tightly against my shoulder.

Lopex and his men had heated the tip again in the rekindled fire, and as they lowered it into the cleft by my cheek I could feel the white heat scorch my ear. "Now walk in and line us up with the eye," Lopex whispered loudly. "Hold it tight until we thrust, then jump off—*fast.*"

My mouth was dry as I crept across its heaving chest until the stake was lined up. It was pointed at the centre of the creature's deep eye socket, a few paces away.

"Now!" The thrust was so strong it knocked the forked stick out of my hands. The stake rubbed painfully against my shoulder as it slid past me, off course and heading for the creature's cheek. Grabbing it with both hands, I braced it on my shoulder and ran the point up its chest. Back on target, the stake slid across the bony rim to dive deep into the socket and plunge into the suddenly opening eyeball.

With a deafening shriek, the creature sat bolt upright. I was thrown off its chest onto a flabby thigh and flipped onto the stone floor, smashing the wind from me. The creature's huge mouth opened and from it sprayed a long, shrill scream like a giant steam kettle. One huge hand reached up and ripped the stake from its eye, flinging it across the cavern. A bloody mixture of steaming ooze erupted from the shattered eyeball, splashing me as I lay stunned on the floor. A huge fist smashed down, missing me by a hand's width. The Cyclops was writhing in agony, its body convulsively heaving off the ground, arms and legs beating furiously against the floor of the cave all around me. I staggered to my feet, put my head down and ran through a maelstrom of flailing limbs.

The Greeks were scattering in all directions, finding holes wherever they could. I was groping along the wall in the gloom when an arm—a human-sized one—reached out from a wide crevice and dragged me in. It was Lopex. "Stay here, boy," he whispered. "Keep still. It's blind, but it can still hear."

I nodded, panting. The creature's screams were subsiding, but it was still thrashing unpredictably. After a few minutes, Lopex spoke.

"You did a good job up there," he said quietly. "How old are you really, boy?"

I was about to protest when I realized that he must know already. "Fifteen. I'm small for my age."

He grunted. "I thought so. No twelve-year-old could do that. Not many adults either." He rubbed his chin through his beard. "My own son Telemachus must be nearly your age. Why did you lie?"

I shrugged. "Would you have let a fifteen-year-old boy live? Ury nearly killed me as it was."

Lopex nodded. "Your sharp tongue does you no good. But I was right to keep you. You keep thinking in a crisis when most men panic, and you've got the healer's touch. You're too useful to lose, Alexi."

I looked sideways toward him, feeling an unexpected

warmth on my face. In the gloom, his silhouette reminded me again of my father.

A pine knot popped in the fire. The Cyclops, now whimpering quietly by the wall, its knees drawn up to its chest, lifted its head.

"Nobah Djee?" it wheezed in the darkness. Lopex said nothing. "Find, I will," it continued. "Then squeeze you hard, your eyes to pop."

Its voice turned suddenly crafty. "Men of Nobah Djee," it called out. "Let you go, if Nobah Djee you bring." It paused, then added, "If bring him not, then eat you all."

Lopex stirred angrily beside me. "Cyclops!" he called out. "I speak for my men. They are as loyal to me as my own sword. Each of them would rather die than betray me."

I stared through the gloom at him, peering intently at the mouth of the crevasse. Was he insane? But there was no time to be angry. A huge hand shot toward us, smashing into the cave wall nearby. The impact showered us with gravel, drawing a howl of pain from the creature as the hand withdrew. I shook my head in disbelief. That mouth of his was going to get him into a lot of trouble. I froze as I recalled where I had heard those words. Was *that* what I was doing? Gods. No wonder I was getting beaten up so much.

The sound of meaty fingertips fumbling across the cave floor drew my eyes in the creature's direction. A vast, pallid hand loomed from the darkness and began groping slowly toward us.

"Get back!" Lopex gestured toward the back of the fissure. I was already scrambling. The firelight didn't reach far, and in the darkness I met the rear wall with a grunt. Lopex arrived and with a mighty shove hoisted me directly up the wall. I dug my fingers into a damp crack, but couldn't find a foothold. My fingers began to ache as Lopex scaled the wall nearby.

The creature's fingernails clicked against the gravel below me as it reached the cave wall. I held my breath. Very slowly, it began to slide up the wall toward my dangling feet.

A ragged fingernail as big as a platter scraped the bottom of my left foot. As I jerked it out of the way, my right hand gave under the strain and I tumbled off the wall to land flat on the creature's bloody knuckles. It whipped its hand over with a jerk, trying to cup me in its palm, but the manoeuvre threw me off and slammed me against the wall, crushing the breath out of me. Four gigantic fingers groped toward me in the gloom.

As I struggled to stand, a pair of feet landed on the ground just in front of my face, the faint firelight reflecting off the inlaid brass on the sandals. With the hand approaching, Lopex whipped his sword from his back and thrust it deep under the creature's middle fingernail.

Its scream was as loud as when we stabbed its eyeball. Lopex was nearly pulled over as the hand jerked back, but he clung to his sword, yanking it out as the hand retreated. He grabbed me under the arm and hauled me upright.

"Run, boy!" he hissed. I staggered out of the fissure, Lopex on my heels. In the main cavern, the dying fire still cast a flickering light on the creature now sucking its wounded finger, its face contorted in pain. Lopex hustled me deeper into the cave, out of reach of those monstrous hands.

"I think it's had enough for tonight," he remarked. "We should be safe for now." But if I'd thought he might explain his reckless outburst up near the cave mouth, I was disappointed. As we reached a patch of pungent straw by the wall, he pointed to a spot nearby and lay down. "Get some rest," he grunted, closing his eyes.

Moaning in its corner, the creature kept me from sleeping again that night, and the early morning bleating of its flocks, anxious to get out, brought any hope of rest to an end. The creature stirred, and a moment later I felt a hand shake my shoulder. It was Lopex.

"Wake up. You're the stealthiest. Go and fetch some grapes from the baskets. I don't want the men on empty stomachs this morning."

He looked at my expression with what was very nearly a grin. "Would you prefer to go back to drudge work? Every skill has its price, Alexias."

As I crept to the front of the cave, I felt a warmth spreading through me. He'd called me Alexias. I wondered for a moment what Mela would have thought of him, then stopped in my tracks. Mela would have reminded me that he was a Greek barbarian, one of the horde who had murdered our father and destroyed our city. I frowned, wondering why that seemed so hard to remember.

Climbing carefully into a boat-sized basket, I picked out several bunches of the creature's huge grapes. As I climbed back out, my foot kicked something hard and metallic. It was a dagger, glinting in the early morning light around the boulder. As I bent to look, I realized it was my sister's. Sophronios must have dropped it when the creature grabbed him. I stared at it for a moment before tucking it into my tunic.

As we ate, the Cyclops sat up, stretched, and reached into the basket I had just left to pull out a handful of grape clusters, scooping grapes, stems and leaves into its maw. It turned to face the bleating beasts around it as it chewed.

"Tend my flocks, no more I can. Left me blind, has Nobah Djee." It paused. "Out to graze, must let you pass, but thieving men, in cave must stay." It sat in thought for a moment, then climbed to its feet and put a shoulder to the boulder.

"Here we go, men," whispered Lopex. "Follow me. Wait for the sheep and slip out with them. Stay absolutely silent. Now, move."

A sliver of light grew to a bright beam as the boulder moved. The Cyclops hadn't corralled its animals last night, and they clustered eagerly around the gap. As we mingled with the sheep milling behind the goats at the entrance, I looked warily up at the creature's face, looming ahead of me like a huge sickly moon as it squatted down beside the opening. Were we sure we'd blinded it? Gods, I hoped so. But the entrance was drawing nearer. In a few moments, I'd be safe.

The sheep were trickling out much too slowly. Something was wrong.

Nearest the entrance, I was the first to spot it. The Cyclops had laid down one giant arm across the opening like a gate. As each sheep approached, it carefully stroked the woolly creature before letting it out. Robbed of its sight, the creature was seeking us by touch.

I turned back, trying to retreat from those crushing fingers, but now drawn by the daylight, the bleating sheep were crowding eagerly forward, pushing me helplessly along with them. Stronger and heavier, the soldiers were wading forcefully back out of the tight-packed flock, but I was being swept ever closer. Unable to make a sound, I waved my arms frantically, trying to catch the eye of a soldier nearby.

He turned and looked directly at me. It was Ury. A cruel smile crept across his lips as he took in the situation. Looking me directly in the eye, he leaned back against the wall and folded his arms.

I glanced back, frantic. The hand was only a few paces away. I pushed hard against the solid mass of sheep, but my bare feet skidded on the stone floor as they bore me forward. The huge hand was finishing with the ram just ahead when an idea came.

Dropping to my back on the floor, I wrapped my arms around the necks of two sheep to either side of me and pulled them together over me. Their sharp front hooves clicked against the stone floor beside my head as they struggled for balance, tugging me along with them toward the light. The massive hand descended, and I buried my arms as deeply as I could in their fleece, hoping the thick fingers wouldn't feel them.

It passed over their backs, brushing my arms through the fleece . . . and stopped. The Cyclops grunted while I held my breath in terror. The hand came back to touch both heads. It stopped again.

I heard it mumble, perplexed. "Two I feel, side by side." It paused, trying to work it out. I was sweating so hard my fingers were losing their grip. In a few seconds it would figure it out, and its fingers would reach down to pluck me from beneath the sheep.

The deep rumble came again. "Afraid they are of Nobah Djee, loose in cave." The light changed as it lifted its arm, and my two sheep staggered out into the morning sunlight, dragging me with them.

Chapter 16

MY GRIP GAVE way just beyond the cave mouth, and I slipped to the ground in the rocky courtyard. The sheep trotted off to join their fellows nearby, bleating happily. For a little while I lay limp on the ground, drinking the fresh hillside breeze and letting the terrified knot in my stomach unwind. Every few moments another sheep issued from the cave mouth and trotted past.

After a little while, I was calm enough to sit up. The Cyclops had a large flock, but I didn't want to be there when it came out after them. I scrambled to my feet, wondering what to do.

A moment later, three sheep came out, trotting side-by-side as though they'd been yoked to a cart. I was peering at them when one of them spoke. "You there! Come here!"

I gaped.

"Not the sheep, boy—down here!"

I looked closer. Beneath the flank of the leftmost sheep was a man's head. It was Deklah. I waited for him to let go, but he didn't.

"Cut me loose," he called. "My knife is in my belt."

As I approached, I realized that he'd been tied underneath the three sheep with grapevines. Grabbing his knife, I sawed away at the woody strands until they let go. As the sheep trotted off, Deklah stood up and started rubbing his arms and legs. Three more sheep staggered out abreast, barely staying upright. Pharos's dark-bearded head protruded from beneath the middle one, his legs trailing conspicuously behind. Deklah snatched the knife from me and headed over.

Over the next short while, three more men emerged blinking into the sunlight, each tied beneath a group of sheep. I looked up to see Pharos nearby. He glanced at me as we watched another set of yoked sheep trotting toward us, a one-eyed soldier named Leonidas strapped beneath. "Very clever, your escape," he remarked. "Ury not helping. I saw."

I glanced up at him. "You saw that?"

He nodded. "Too far for helping. And Ury helping only himself. He and his cousins from Chefalonos, lying always, stealing from others, returning nothing."

"Those friends of his—they're his cousins?" I asked.

Pharos nodded, watching Deklah cutting Leonidas loose. "Cousins are they all. And not just they." He rubbed his arms where the tightly-tied vines had cut into them. "Pharos, too, is cousin to Eurylochos."

There was a long delay before the next set of bound sheep emerged. When they did, it was Ury himself underneath them. As he was cut loose, he scrambled up, glancing nervously back toward the cave, before turning and catching sight of the rest of us.

"What are you stupid *methusai* standing around for?" he cursed. "We have to be off the beach and under sail before that thing figures out we've escaped. Now get moving!"

To my surprise, it was Deklah who shook his head. "But Ury, Lopex is still in there! We have to stay. He might need help."

Ury stared at him in disbelief. "Were you asleep when that thing ate Sophro and Bolos? Do you want to be next? With Lopex gone, I'm in command, and I say move!"

A big hand fell on his shoulder. "Pharos is not leaving Lopex. His thinking is more needed than yours, Eurylochos."

Ury shook Pharos's hand off. "Thinking? You don't even know what the word means, you big stupid ape." He looked around at us. "By Zeus, are all of you idiots? That creature will be out here any moment!"

Especially if he kept yelling. Ury looked around at the men's expressions and his voice took on a wheedling tone.

"Look, Lopex can take care of himself. He'd tell you the same thing. Or did you forget it's his fault we were in there?"

But Deklah shook his head again, his jaw set. "Do you think I want to be eaten? But you know, Lopex did get us out of there. Maybe it's different for you, but I have to stay." He marched off toward the cave mouth. Pharos followed him, and, after a pause, the rest of us did too.

"Now what?" Ury stumped up as we huddled behind the boulder. "How long are you going to wait? Or are you going to march in and rescue him?"

Leaning out from behind the boulder, Deklah waved him to silence. "Listen. It's saying something."

We crept toward the entrance. The creature's low voice rumbled from inside. "Always leading, head of flock. But not today, find you at back."

We crept through the stone courtyard to the cave mouth and peered inside. A few paces from the entrance, the Cyclops's gory head was bent down as it spoke to something behind its arm.

Its other hand reached down and hoisted the creature into the air. It was a massive old ram, the largest of the flock. I gasped. Dangling beneath it, his knuckles white as he clung to the ram's curling horns, was Lopex.

The Cyclops lifted it to its face as a man might lift a mouse, a milky fluid leaking from its shattered eyeball. There was a black patch under the fingernail that Lopex had stabbed. The ram kicked frantically, terrified by the unaccustomed height and the heavy weight on its horns.

"Take your eye, to see again," the Cyclops rumbled. "Nobah Djee, then could I find." A frown crossed its brow. "Why so heavy, O my ram? Too much weight, for lonely beast."

It brought the struggling creature closer, turning it this way and that as if trying to catch a glimpse through some undamaged corner of its shattered eye. Lopex's body twisted only a foot from the creature's mouth, his billowing purple cloak nearly brushing its cheek. Kicking in terror, the ram was savaging Lopex's face with its sharp hooves, Lopex's teeth bared in a fierce grimace as he struggled to avoid them.

I snatched up an egg-sized stone. I had to do this right— there was only time to do it once. Drawing my arm back, I aimed by memory for the alcove where I had seen the giant knife, and threw the stone carefully into the cave. It arced up over the creature's legs and smashed loudly against the huge bronze tool. The Cyclops jerked its head up at the noise, its face darkening. "Thieves in cave now stealing knife," it rumbled. It set the ram down at the cave mouth and turned to grope on the floor inside.

Lopex let go of the ram's horns and collapsed just inside the gap. Freed, the ram scrambled out. After a moment, Lopex staggered to his feet and followed it. A long gash beneath his eye was dripping blood onto his slashed tunic, torn and bloodstained in a dozen places. As he caught sight of us, he straightened up and wiped the blood from his face.

Ury shouldered me out of the way. "Thank the gods you're okay, Lopex. That thing will be out at any moment!"

Lopex wiped the welling blood from his forehead with the hem of his tunic. "Believe me, it's good to see you too." He paused to catch his breath, then peered at Ury. "That was an excellent idea, escaping under the sheep. I'm surprised. I've never looked to you for ideas before, Ury."

I opened my mouth angrily, but there was a grunt from the cave. The boulder was moving. Lopex put a finger to his lips and beckoned us out of the courtyard.

Behind us, the Cyclops had shouldered its way out and was following its bleating flocks. Even blind, it was walking faster than we were. Lopex glanced back.

"Run!" he mouthed, gesturing down the hill. I set off as fast as I could, my limp still slowing me. The rest of the men sprinted ahead, dodging the rubble that littered the slope to head along the gully to the beach where our ship lay.

The crew were sitting in groups finishing breakfast, and just ahead of me Ury rolled in among them like an avalanche. "Drop what you're doing! Push that ship out! Break camp! There's a Cyclops coming!" he yelled.

Confusion erupted. Most of the men probably didn't know what a Cyclops was, but Ury's tone told them all they needed. They began dashing everywhere, some snatching at tents, food and stores and getting in each other's way while others ran to push the ship off the beach, tripping in their haste. Their noise swelled rapidly as I reached the camp.

Lopex limped in last. Taking in the scene instantly, he swung up onto the stern deck. "Achaeans! Listen to me! There is no reason for fear. It is true there is a Cyclops on this island. But if we remain silent it can never find us: last night as it slept, I blinded it with a stake through its eye. So hold your tongues and prepare the ship for sea—*quietly*. We will sail once the ship is reloaded."

Reassured, the men who had begun dashing around at Ury's shout calmed down and began stowing supplies on board, Lopex supervising from the bow. I was refuelling the fire pots when he appeared at my shoulder and shook his head, wrinkling his nose. I nodded and put them out— smoke could give us away as easily as noise.

On the beach, the cooking fire had already been smothered, and the tripods and pots were being collected. While thirty men heaved the ship out into the shallows, others, guided by gestures from Lopex, were loading some sheep that had trailed down the hill behind us. I grinned. Even in an emergency, the man was an opportunist.

As I collected a bundle of sleeping blankets, there was a tap on my shoulder. I turned to see Pen, smiling shyly. "Alexi!" he whispered. "You're back! What happened? Is it true, there's a, what is it, a *Cyclops*? What's that?"

I was surprised at how pleased I was to see him. He was standing easily, his bandaged leg causing no pain. A clean bandage, recently changed, I noted. "I'll tell you sometime," I whispered back. "Right now we really have to get off the beach." I pointed. "Fetch those cess trench shovels. Don't let them clink." He nodded happily and trotted off. Something had shifted in our relationship, and it seemed natural for me to tell him what to do.

I began to splash out to the stern ladder with my load, but stopped. There was a terrible sound coming nearer. A ponderous thudding like someone slowly pounding the ground with a huge mallet. My face went cold. I turned to look, and the pale head of the Cyclops appeared over the lip of the gully.

Chapter 17

IT WAS WALKING slowly in our direction, pounding the ground with the stripped white trunk of a dead pine tree as it came. We froze, all eyes turning automatically to Lopex. He gestured to stop where we were, and we watched, motionless, as the creature tapped its way along the gully toward the beach.

Broad daylight revealed the full horror of its appearance. Its skin was a blotchy white, and its eye socket, now partly scabbed over, was leaking blood and yellow pus down its face. It emerged from the gully onto the beach, then stopped and sniffed the air.

"Find you soon, Nobah Djee," I heard it muttering. "Gone

for now but soon to eat." It continued out of the gully onto the beach, heading directly into the camp. The soldiers crept out of its path as it advanced, moving aside tools and weapons, anything that might alert it to the camp around it.

Near the centre of the campsite, the creature suddenly changed direction. I felt a chill as I spotted the brass cooking tripod directly in its path. Once that huge foot touched it, the Cyclops would know instantly that we were here.

A soldier crept out. Deklah. A massive foot crushed down only a few paces from him, but he kept going, weaving his way directly between those vast feet. Holding the tripod gently to keep the legs from clanking, he picked it up and tiptoed out of the creature's way, the tree-trunk cane smashing a deep depression into the sand right next to him. I let my breath out slowly. He might have been a complainer, but in bravery he could stand with Lopex.

The Cyclops shambled down to the water's edge, its pine cane pounding large uneven circles in the wet beach sand, pausing several times to sniff the air. Lopex stood on deck, gripping the rail and watching the creature intently for any sign that it was about to move toward the ship. After a few moments, it turned the other way and shuffled off. The beach ended at a rocky spit that jutted into the ocean a short distance away, and the creature turned and began stumping its way along it.

Lopex gestured for the men to continue, and a short time later we pushed the ship into deeper water. The Cyclops was sitting quietly at the end of the spit, its face in its hands. Standing in the stern where they could see him, Lopex signalled to the men, who extended their oars and began rowing, timed by his slow gestures. A short distance out, they turned the ship by poling off the bottom.

As I watched from the stern, I realized with alarm that our course would take us close to where the Cyclops was sitting.

"Is he crazy? What's Lopex doing?" I whispered to Zanthos, who was leaning on his steering oar.

Zanthos pointed. "You see where the water gets all small and flat there? Just there to port?" he whispered back. "Means a sandbar down below. Can see her when tide's out, most likely. But we can't slide over her, keel's too deep. Got to come around by this side, see?" I nodded.

As we approached, I heard the creature muttering to itself through its huge hands. "Meant to happen, this was not. Foretold to lose my eye, my sight, to brazen hero, proud and tall. Not to band of creeping dwarfs." It lifted its head, and what might have been a tear ran down its giant cheek. "Wrong, it was, the oracle," it groaned. "Betrayed was I. Came how to this?"

We were coming up on the creature now, and Lopex signalled the men to stop rowing. Our momentum carried us forward, and as we slid silently past, he went to the stern railing to look up at it. His knuckles gleamed white as he clenched the rail, his teeth bared.

The men sat perfectly still as we drifted beneath the creature's eyeless gaze. Could it guess we were nearby? But it just sat, making strange choking noises as we drew farther away. We had escaped.

Then, to my astonishment, Lopex called out.

"Cyclops!" he cried, his voice mocking. "You have taken my men to fill your belly for a day, but I have taken your sight forever! Perhaps next time you will receive guests with the honour they are due!" He turned on his heel and barked at the men. "Now row!"

But the Cyclops had scrambled to its feet the moment it heard Lopex's voice. Groping in the shallows, it hefted a boulder half the size of our ship and lobbed it in our direction. I gripped the rail fearfully, but the rock hissed over our heads and splashed into the sea ahead.

A moment later, the bow of the ship was wrenched up as if by a giant hand, spilling the men from their rowing benches and knocking me to the deck. The boulder had triggered a huge wave that was driving us directly back toward the island. A few men cried out, but their companions stopped them, pointing. I looked up to see us being washed straight toward the Cyclops, now standing just offshore, knee-deep in the water. It was turning its vast head slowly back and forth, listening. Sniffing.

The *Pelagios* had slipped sideways as the wave swept us toward the creature. In a few moments, we would wash up against one of those enormous legs. I clutched the rail in terror as we drifted toward it.

Lopex wasn't idle. Unlacing the nearest oar from its leather stay, he leaned over the railing with it. As we drifted closer, he threaded it silently between the creature's legs. The outstretched oar almost brushed its left shin as it nosed silently up against the wet, seaweed-coated rocks behind. We were so close that the near-side rowers were underneath its hairy, overhanging belly. If it moved its arm, or took a step forward . . . I couldn't look at it, couldn't look away.

Lopex strained in eerie silence, pushing hard against his oar, feet braced against the slippery deck. Our slow drift stopped, so close that the nearest rowers could have reached over the rail and touched the creature's hairy legs. Seeing his plan, several men carefully unlaced their oars and began to help. Directly above us, the Cyclops's head continued to turn back and forth.

Very slowly, our ship began to move again, back out to sea. With infinite caution, Lopex used his long oar to pole us along the bottom, the sinews of his arms standing out with the strain. A little farther out, Lopex gave the sign to untangle the remaining oars, and once more we began to row.

We had pulled a little farther out when, to my astonishment, Lopex shouted once again. "Creature! Why hunt what you cannot see? Your pebbles cannot reach me, but I can still strike you with my voice. Save your energy to gather your sheep, if we have left you any."

The Cyclops whipped its head around and opened its mouth. "O my kin!" it cried, its voice impossibly loud. "For help I call! Gored am I, bereft of sight! Robbed, my grotto, flocks are gone! Punish him, who stole my sight!"

Vast voices boomed back across the water. At least one was coming from the island dead ahead. "Your eye?" "Your sheep?" "How can this be?" "Reveal his name, revenge to bring!"

The Cyclops replied in that same ear-splitting bellow. "This and more, has Nobah Djee! Nobah Djee has blinded me!"

There was a brief pause before the distant voices replied, decidedly grumpier. "Done all this, has *nobody*? Sick in head, or mad, are you! If harmed are you by *nobody*, then let *nobody* heal you now! Alone, leave us, your bed to seek. Tomorrow, wiser may you be."

The Cyclops stood for a moment, speechless with rage and confusion. A roar of laughter swelled from the men, and I was reminded once again how clever my master was. It was clear why they had nicknamed him "the fox."

Now Deklah called out from his oar, grinning. "Creature! Didn't your father teach you to *fear nobody*? Now you know who he was talking about!" Several of the men laughed so hard that some lost their grip on their oars, entangling the others. But we were beyond the reach of boulders now, and Lopex called out a parting shot.

"Do you wish to know who destroyed you? Very well, eater of guests. My true name is Odysseus, son of Laertes, ruler of Ithaca!"

The creature shook itself and straightened up. "Hear my curse, Odysseus!" Its voice boomed across the water. "Listen well, O thief of sight! Long and long to plough the waves, before your Ithaca you reach! Sunk, your ship and gone, your spoil; dead, your men and aged, your brow. And if at last your home you see, a lone and nameless beggar be! In my father's name, I beg—Poseidon mighty, hear my plight!" As the creature finished, it opened its arms wide to the ocean, blind face to the sky. A deep rumble rolled back across the waves, as though the ocean itself had replied.

Odysseus! I'd thought of my master as Lopex for so long I had nearly forgotten who he really was. Odysseus the trickster, as we called him in Troy. Wiliest of the Greeks. For someone that clever, giving the Cyclops his name had been foolish. To curse someone, you had to know their name. Not that it mattered. We were headed for Ithaca again, wherever that was, and Odysseus would have his own heal-ers there. I'd be just a slave again, most likely being worked slowly to death myself.

"Alexi!"

It was Odysseus, crossing the stern deck toward me. "Go below and check for leaks. That last wave may have loosened some planks. Set the slaves to bailing if you have to." He didn't seem even to have heard the Cyclops's curse. I headed for the stern hold ladder, but Odysseus stopped me with a hand on my arm. "Deklah told me how your stone helped me escape that thing." he said. "I won't forget that."

The wave from the boulder had shaken up both the cargo and the slaves in the hold, but the hull planks were still tight. Kassander, Zosimea and the other two slaves were lying in the far point of the stern, bracing themselves in case the ship bucked again. Kassander was bleeding from a cut on his forehead, Zosimea cradling one arm.

"Alexi?" Seeing me, Kassander scrambled up. "What happened up there?"

All the anger I felt at being lied to came welling back up. I was about to climb back up the hold ladder but turned back. The other slaves needed to know. "It was that thing. It was trying to catch us. We're out of reach now." I was partway up the ladder when he spoke again.

"Alexi. I know you don't trust me. But I may have some information for you."

I kept going but his next sentence stopped me cold. "It's about your sister."

I turned. "What about her?"

He beckoned and I came down slowly. "Well?"

He took my shoulder and led me away from the other slaves. "Tell me, did your sister . . . die by being thrown down some steps?"

I nodded mutely, feeling my chest tighten.

"Then listen." He lowered his voice. "Last night I overheard two soldiers at the cess trench. Takis was asking how Sophronios got that terrible gash on his nose. Apparently the other soldier saw it. The night of the invasion, after Ury's brother went down, Sophronios showed up in the lane. He saw a Trojan girl lying dead nearby. Being Sophronios, he went over to take whatever she might have left to offer. But when he pulled at her tunic, she sat up and slashed his face, cutting deep into his nose. Sophro twisted her arm and she dropped the knife but got free. She ran off."

"Liar!" I shouted, furious. "Sophronios told me what really happened! He said he found her and cut her throat! Get away from me, you *Greek*!"

Kassander glanced around uneasily. "Keep it down, Alexi. You know what will happen if they discover me."

"That's too bad," I said coldly. "You've lied since I met you and you're lying now."

Kassander paused. "Wait," he said suddenly. "He also said something about . . . a well. That was it. She was lying against a well."

I opened my mouth but nothing came out. She *had* been lying by a well. I'd seen her clearly in the torchlight. Still— "I don't believe you," I replied, feeling less certain. As I turned and climbed back up the ladder, Kassander called softly after me. "Alexi. Yes, I lied about who I was. But if you think about it, I've never betrayed your trust. You'll have to decide who you believe."

Back on deck, I sagged against the stern railing. We were in the channel between the islands now, far enough offshore to pick up a breeze. From amidships came half-hearted curses as the men struggled to raise the mast. I hardly heard them, consumed by Kassander's words. Was there a chance he was telling the truth?

I straightened up and leaned over the rail to look forward. The bright sunlight sparkling off the waves made it hard to see where we were headed. But for me, it was suddenly clear. If it took the rest of my life, I would find out what had become of my sister.

ABOUT THE AUTHOR

 Greek mythology has fascinated me since I discovered a copy of *Bulfinch's Mythology* in my father's library as a child. All the same, my writing career took a twenty-year detour through software development before I was able to become a full-time writer and spend more time at home raising my daughters, Kathleen and Anitra. I started with Homer's *Odyssey* because it's a classic story, but one that nowadays is usually read only in university courses. I decided to create a version that young people would read for fun: a realistic adventure, told not by the traditional heroes but by an outsider. For centuries, readers have been seeing the destruction of Troy through the eyes of the Greeks; I felt it was time to see that event through the eyes of a Trojan. My family and I live in Toronto, where the winters are growing steadily milder and the summers muggier. We have no dog.

DON'T MISS THE THRILLING
SEQUEL TO *TORN FROM TROY*

THE
SEA GOD'S
CURSE

Fresh from the clutches
of the Cyclops, Alexi and his
captors confront the cannibal
ship-eaters, the wrath of the
unchained elements and the
domain of the dead as they
struggle homeward.

TO READ THE FIRST CHAPTERS OF
THE SEA GOD'S CURSE, VISIT

patrickbowman.ca